monsoonbooks

MW01675377

DOG CATCHER

Erich R. Sysak first learned about greyhound racing while working as a veterinary technician in Tampa, Florida.

Today, he lives on the gulf coast of Thailand in Cha-am. He teaches writing at an international university, cultivates orchids and studies Siamese history.

His articles and short stories appear in the *Bangkok Post*, *Paumanok Review*, *Oxford Magazine*, *Rare Book Review* and the *Nation* newspaper among others.

DOG CATCHER

Erich R. Sysak

monsoon

monsoonbooks

Published in 2006
by Monsoon Books Pte Ltd
Blk 106 Jalan Hang Jebat #02–14
Singapore 139527
www.monsoonbooks.com.sg

ISBN-13: 798-981-05-3374-8
ISBN-10: 981-05-3374-8

This is a work of fiction, and any resemblance to actual events, locales, or persons, living or dead, is merely coincidental.

Printed in Singapore

10 09 08 07 06   1 2 3 4 5 6 7 8 9

Chapter 1

I opened the heavy lid of the freezer, and hooked it to a chain that was bolted to the cement wall. The freezer reminded me of a coffin, and in a way it was. The steam rose from inside. The cool air blew across my sweaty face. I looked inside and counted eight full trash bags.

I set my clipboard on a washing machine next to the cooler, then propped open the back door with a block of wood they kept outside. The back door opened to a fenced enclosure about twelve by ten feet. Its floor was made of cement, stained with rust-colored spots from the dogs that spent part of their day outside in the sunshine just below the I-75 overpass that snaked its way from Scott Road to Central Avenue.

I heard the steady rumble of cars and trucks barreling overhead. I tasted the tar and smoke and gasoline in the air. It was a hot, lonely place for the dogs to spend their lives, but they were just dogs, and I didn't have any say in the matter.

Dr. Fielding ran the hospital. He'd been a veterinarian long before I'd become an Animal Control officer, and that was seven years.

I had watched Dr. Fielding perform miracles. He'd brought a flea-infested Persian cat back to life right in front of my eyes. He had twisted his long fingers into the cat's blue mouth and pried at something deep within. His eyes screwed up, and looked over the surgical light that hung from the ceiling like a mechanical arm. What he looked at I didn't know and never would really. But whatever it was, it must have given him the insight to pluck and pinch life into a dead cat. I knew many veterinarians, but only Dr. Fielding could look off into space somewhere and see life's blueprint.

I hefted one of the heavy trash bags from the freezer and slung it over my shoulder. A frozen skull cracked against my shoulder. The cold sank into my cheek, and the smell lingered in my throat. The smell was like dirt after a heavy rain, packed, moist, things from underneath dredged up and steaming in the sun. I carried the body outside and tossed it into the open bed of a green '72 Ford pickup. I used the truck every Tuesday morning for my route. After the body tour, I went to lunch at Greenhorns, then traded the Ford for my truck that I used the rest of the day to answer calls. I never got used to the thud the bodies made when they hit the steel of the truck bed. I slid the bag to the back to make room for the others.

The bad thing about the Ford was that by the end of the route some of the bodies thawed out; the bed was open to the Palm County sun, and the heat was worse somehow when you were on the road. When a body thawed out, the bag filled with water and locked in the smell. When I dug the bags out of the truck to throw into the incinerator at the kennel, the water spilled and the smell stayed on me the rest of the day. I changed shirts, I took showers, I sprinkled Old Spice over my face and chest, but the smell stayed.

I loaded all eight bags, slammed the tailgate, and latched it so it wouldn't pop open from a hard ride. I went inside and walked through the damp hallway of Dr. Fielding's hospital to a tub and washed my hands. I dried my hands and went into the next room, where the greyhounds lived. I watched them wedge their long snouts through the cage wires. They were barrel-chested, muscular, and shy. Lying on the cement floor all day rubbed the fur on their legs and chests to dull, silver patches that looked bright against their dark coats.

Dr. Fielding took blood from them for other dogs who were anemic. I had never asked, but supposed he got them from trainers and breeders, then kept them until he found someone willing to adopt. There was a new batch of greyhounds in his hospital about every two months.

The two there now had both been racers. I knew by the numbered tattoos in their ears, but they must have been slow or stubborn or both because they had ended up here. I lifted the tucked ear of the brindle male and looked at the tattoo.

The greyhound trainers and breeders usually had a dog put to sleep if it couldn't race or follow instructions. Some used vets; others did the job themselves. It didn't matter if the dog was young or healthy. The trainers didn't want another kennel to get hold of their dogs and breed them, so they made sure that a dog was dead before they would pay the bill. Some of the vets would do it for the money, some wouldn't. I sure as hell wouldn't have done it if I were a vet, but then there were a lot of things I didn't like about the business. I knew some greyhound farms killed up to three hundred dogs a month. Only a few dogs ended up as racers. The rest cost too much to feed.

The greyhounds' cage was chest high, with a slab of plywood over the top. In the cage was a torn wool blanket and a red bucket filled with water. The cage was just big enough for them to take four or five steps in any direction, but they were used to it. Greyhounds spent most of their lives in cages.

They were good dogs, and I loved to see them race. I never made much money betting on them, but then the game wasn't made for people to make money. The owners and the state of Florida made the money. I had never met an owner. I'd seen their names in the racing forms and sometimes in the newspaper, but I'd never met one in person.

Dr. Fielding's office was behind the X-ray machine in a dark room that had a kitchen, a television, and a couple of worn couches. I sat on a couch, and filled out the body slip. I wrote that I had carried four dogs to my truck, though I had actually carried eight. I had a little deal with some of the veterinarians. Animal Control charged six dollars per body, whether it was a five-pound cat or a ninety-pound St. Bernard. The veterinarians were required by law to dispose of the bodies through an approved agent. Animal Control was the cheapest agent in the county. With a few select vets I cut the number on the official slip to half. That way, I made a little and the vet saved a little when we split the difference under the table. Since I was the one who had to toss them into the incinerator, I was the only one who knew the actual number, the body count.

That day I had made one hundred and two dollars from Dr. Fielding and a few others. I made close to that amount every week and socked it away on Friday at the Barnett Bank near my trailer.

It felt strange to me, even though the animals were dead and I'd had nothing to do with how or why. Somebody had to do it. Somebody had to haul off the dogs and cats and coons and foxes that were hit by cars or found dead or diseased or put to sleep because of age. Still, it felt strange.

Dr. Fielding walked into the office. He wore a long, white lab coat with the blue name tag over the right chest pocket. He was a tall man, over six and a half feet. He ducked under the top of the door frame. His hair was curly on the sides and thinning at the top, and he wore gold-rimmed glasses that slipped down the bridge of his long nose.

"Morning, Legget." He walked around the couch to his desk, sat behind it and opened the top drawer.

"Got eight all together. Four on the slip, so you owe me for four. That's thirty-six dollars if you don't care to do your math. How are my hounds doing?"

He slipped the money across the top of his desk, then leaned back in his chair. "Just fine. When do you want to take one home?"

"You ask me that every time, and I tell you: I live in a trailer. I can't have a dog. I'd have to throw out my bed just to make room."

He nodded, then unwrapped a piece of spearmint gum. I smelled it. Chewing slowly, carefully, he folded his hands and leaned back. "You've been a dog catcher a long time, but still you haven't seen everything. You're due."

He snapped his gum and winked. Doc talked that way often enough. I smiled as if I was in on the joke and got my papers together, stood up. We shook hands, and as I walked down the hallway to my truck, I heard the cabinet open and the familiar clank of a whiskey bottle against a glass. Dr. Fielding had told me he could've been governor if he'd wanted, if he hadn't become a vet. Veterinarians didn't get the same respect as people doctors, even though he said people were easier to treat. Animals couldn't say what hurt or how a medicine made them feel, and there were thousands of species. Every species had its own problems and cures. But he was a doctor, and I wasn't. Second in his class at the state university. He knew people, politicians, lawyers. People knew him. That made a lot of difference in my world. Veterinarians enjoyed a privilege that an Animal Control officer could respect or attempt to destroy, but never ignore. And Dr. Fielding was the most powerful man I knew.

* * *

I drove around the back of Animal Control, through a tall chain link fence with three strands of barbed wire across the top. The incinerator was in a small field of Bahia grass with a few palm trees, down a worn dirt path. It looked like an oversized dumpster with a twenty-foot smokestack. About thirty feet from the machine the smell of burnt plastic and flesh hit you like a brick. The smoke that came out of the machine was toxic, and everybody knew it, but nobody wanted to tear out every dog from every plastic bag. So we just tossed everything in the way it came.

I backed the pickup to the wooden gate that was open and hanging on its last two-by-four from all the times I, and other officers, had backed into it. I dropped the tailgate and hauled out the first bag. Of course it had melted, and a healthy splash of cold, reeking water slopped across my shirt. The shirt glued itself to my chest, but I kept moving. The best way to finish was to keep pushing until the last bag was in the fire. I tossed the bags into the incinerator, flicked it on and closed up the truck. The pickup would wait there till next week.

Inside the kennel, the dogs erupted with barks and yelps. There was no way to get used to the noise thirty dogs could make. You couldn't talk loud enough to hear your own voice. And there was no sense in yelling at them.

Our kennel was old and made of cement. Cement gutters ran in front of the cages. Kennel attendants went back there twice a day with rubber boots and hoses to spray them out. Thirty dogs produced a lot of waste. The kennel attendants cleaned it twice a day, and John Leland had to keep on their backs like a lion just to get it done right.

Animal Control, like any county service that lived off taxes, was always hurting. We could only afford two, sometimes three people to work the kennels, and it was a big job. People quit in a few days or weeks because it was just too much work for a few underpaid and sore hands.

The walls of the kennel had been painted a hundred times, red, blue, yellow, white. But the acid from the urine and the claws and constant rubbing against the sides had given it a beaten, dirty look. It looked like buckets of hot bleach had been thrown at the walls, leaving patches of white over red under yellow, like a bad quilt.

I walked into the dark kitchen and washed my hands and arms and face in a huge steel sink filled with dirty bowls. The dog and cat food was stacked against the wall, fifty-pound bags of dry pellets. I slapped the side of a new, stuffed bag. It was like hard flesh, and I liked the sound. The animals settled when they realized I wasn't there to feed them. I didn't see the kennel attendants and wondered if they were smoking pot again. John would fire them if he found out.

I went out the side of the building, where I had parked my truck. The kennel attendants were there behind a tree. When they heard the door pop shut behind me, they peeked around the tree where my truck was parked. Tom, a skinny high school kid, looked me in the eye and coughed.

Albert was heavy, about eighteen or nineteen. He had a clump of blond hair and freckles. He wore a black rubber apron and rubber boots. He looked wet and wrinkled like a prune. Tom was paper thin. When I looked at him, I thought of chalk dust in a strong breeze. He was nothing.

"How's the kennel looking, fellas?" I unhooked my keys from my belt and walked toward the truck.

"OK," Tom said, and snarled a little.

I wasn't scared of them. I was big enough to keep them at arm's length. Luckily, I was trim and twenty-five and tall. The job helped. Chasing animals through backyards and woods and streets built muscles and stamina.

Tom put his hands in his pockets and kicked at the dirt around the thick roots of the oak tree. "Give me a cigar, Legget."

I patted my shirt pocket. "Don't have any to spare."

Albert laughed, and I didn't get the joke. Hell, I didn't get any of their jokes.

"You boys been fiddling with my truck?"

"That piece of shit? Fuck no," Tom said. He was the leader. Albert just slunk behind him and jeered at Tom's smart-ass remarks. Albert was older than Tom, but Tom was smarter and trouble free. Albert had been sent to us by the courts—community service for stealing a car. Turned out the car belonged to his mother's boyfriend, and his parents were trying to teach Albert a lesson.

John liked to be involved in things like that. He wanted to be part of the community and contribute. He didn't talk about it much. He didn't seem to want a pat on the back or anything, but he did things like hiring Albert. Fact was, he was probably better off without him.

I opened the door to my truck and put one boot on the running board. I stared at Tom, let a second or so pass in silence. "Don't let John catch you boys smoking that shit around here."

Tom looked at the ground and waved Albert back to the kennel. I hoped I'd done the right thing.

I started my truck, felt under the seat for my bag, and dug out a clean shirt. The CB coughed static as I hailed Molly. She was sitting in her damp office in the building I had just left. She talked too much, cut her hair short, and dyed it red. Her office was a small job near John's, with a window-unit air conditioner that rattled. When I talked to her on the CB, I had to listen to the clanking in the background. We had to repeat everything at least once. But Molly wouldn't part with her air conditioner. She had said she'd quit if it went. I couldn't blame her. The office got real hot, and the humidity could kill a roach.

John Leland was a thirty-six-year-old black man with an army haircut, a close-cropped beard, broad shoulders like a linebacker, and a disposition like a frontier school teacher. He laughed and gave advice and bought beers as freely as a gambler on a winning streak.

John and I had beers and lunch at Greenhorns every Tuesday. John ate half a chicken sandwich with one Pabst, then wrapped the other half in wax paper to take home to his wife, Beth.

Greenhorns was a small restaurant that people claimed had once served judges, senators, wrestlers, pro baseball players, and models.

The waitresses wore copper uniforms that matched the furniture and wallpaper. They served coffee by the pot, and cold beer if you asked. John and I had picked Greenhorns because it was close to the kennel, and when we'd first started coming, it had the prettiest waitresses in town.

I parked my truck in the back, got the mobile phone from the glove compartment, and went inside. John was sitting in a booth near the back. He was the only black man in the restaurant. He had papers scattered on the table, and was bent over, a red pen in his hand, jotting notes. He had a steaming cup of coffee on the table. There was an empty cup on my side.

"Hey, Legget." He didn't look up from his papers.

"Afternoon, boss."

"I'll get this stuff out of your way in just a second." He looked up. His eyes were red and sleepy. "What do you think?"

"About what?"

John lifted the page he had been writing on, and cleared his throat. "I'm writing a letter to the county commissioner. I'm trying to appeal to his sympathetic side. Puppies and kittens. What do you think, Dear Sir or Your Royal Majesty?"

I poured coffee into my cup and set my phone next to the salt shaker.

"I ordered for you already," John said.

I lit a cigar and leaned back. John borrowed a drag from it, then wadded up the letter.

"Let's have a beer." He waved for the waitress. "How was body tour?"

John didn't know that I grafted money from his organization. If he'd known, he probably would have taken me outside, thrown some fists, then fired me. John knew his dog catchers were not the most honorable, up-standing citizens in the state, but we were all he had, and there was a job to do, and the job never ended. John didn't have time to catch up on things in the street. He kept a small transistor radio in his office. He tuned it to a twenty-four-hour news and weather station. If he heard that a storm was coming, he'd send a message over the CB through Molly, to all the catchers. If you were out there you could see it was going to rain, but that was John. He wanted to be part of things. He was like a father who didn't know how to talk to his kids because he lived in a world of papers and forms, county officials and summons, rabies tags and veterinarians.

"Fine. Dr. Fielding said hello." I lied because John was fond of Dr. Fielding. He believed that Dr. Fielding was a good old boy.

According to John there were new vets and old boys. The old boys had learned medicine the old-fashioned way. The old boys listened to the owners, maybe felt the patient's ribs or looked at its tongue, but they knew what was wrong mostly from experience. The old boys had reduced medicine to a simple proposition: no fancy blood tests or X-rays (unless there was no alternative), and definitely no fancy drugs.

According to John the new vets were detail fanatics. They did every blood, skin, eye, ear, cough and urine test the client would pay for. They piled all the information on a desk or in front of the broke, confused client, then connected things like the pieces of a puzzle. Either way, the results were the same. You could choose an old boy who didn't test or fuss, who lacked ceremony and two-dollar words, but who didn't go as far as one might want him to. The old boy might say, "He can't piss," where the new vet would diagnose your cat's "feline urological syndrome." I liked the old-boy style. Maybe that was something I'd picked up from John.

The waitress came with her tray. An omelette for me and the chicken sandwich with steak fries for John. John wiped the table clean of papers, and the waitress set our plates down. I ordered the beers.

"Are you tired?" I poured myself fresh coffee.

John rolled a fry in a pile of ketchup. "It's my back. Can't get to sleep without whiskey or the damned TV."

"The letter's a good idea."

"No it isn't."

"Why not?"

"Because I've written three, maybe four, and I always get a real nice one back, but it doesn't say anything. I don't know. They're not giving us any more money unless something terrible happens. Then they'll send money, and there'll be ten white boys in suits right behind it asking all sorts of questions."

My mobile phone rang. It was Molly. I pulled a pen from my front pocket and wrote directions on a paper napkin. Sheriff Dario had requested me to a call, but hadn't said what for.

I turned off the phone and clenched the napkin in my fist. John waved me off.

Chapter 2

Dario stood in the driveway with his thumb hooked in the holster at his belt. He pulled up the belt, spit and walked over.

"Afternoon, Legget."

"Afternoon. What's going on?"

"The dog bit an officer while we were searching the house. Took his whole goddamn thumb off."

"Where is it?" I put my thumb in the air.

"Thumb or the dog?"

"Dog," I said.

Dario pointed at the garage door.

"No tag?"

Dario raised his hands. "She claims she lost it."

"Right ..."

The sheriff's department wouldn't touch an animal unless they had to. As far as they were concerned it was Animal Control's problem. Dario wasn't much different, even though we knew each other. I walked to the garage and peeked in. Dario followed. Since the dog had bitten an officer, it would have to be quarantined for thirty days at the kennel. Though it was unlikely the dog had rabies, it didn't have a tag, which probably meant it had no vaccines.

The door bucked out and lifted a few inches off the ground. The dog's head poked under. He was big by the size of the head, about eighty pounds.

"He looks big."

Dario nodded. "What do you want to do?"

I walked to the side of the garage and looked in the door. The room was dark. There was a car in the middle, washer and dryer behind it, a lawnmower, and another door led into the house. I didn't see the dog. Dario stood behind me. He plucked a blade of grass, put it in his mouth and chewed.

"Do you know anything about the dog?"

"Not really, I think it's a Husky."

"Can you get another deputy out here?" I walked back to the truck to get my rabies pole.

Dario came back with another officer, a woman with aviator glasses and a starched uniform. An ambulance arrived and the injured officer walked to it. Dario followed me to the side of the garage. He took off his gun belt and hooked it on a window sill. The woman stood with Dario and waited.

Inside, the garage smelled like onions. I crouched and looked under the car. I saw the dog on the other side. His head lifted and his ears cocked back. They were thick; his fur was thick and brown. There was a white flash of tooth below the wet, black nose.

I walked around the car. My boots squeaked, and the dog turned his eye on me. He needed to see what he was going to bite. A dog always had to look first, then bite. It was a Siberian Husky, and I was surprised it was vicious. They were usually good, calm dogs.

The best way to catch a dog was to let it do the work. I had my rabies pole. It was made of aluminum and plastic, with a wire noose looped at the end. I could pull the wire and snap the noose shut around the dog's head. The way to do it was hold it out at a little angle to the body, kind of like a fishing pole, and just let it hang there like it was nothing important. Let the dog think it was nothing.

The Husky stepped back, and I stepped forward. His tail touched the garage door. There was no room for him to back up. He turned his wedge-shaped head around, then turned back and showed me a little tooth. I moved the noose toward his whiskers, inches from his snout and nose. He stiffened and eyed the noose, but didn't bite. I gave the noose a little twist to make it flop over and tag him on the snout. He took the bait and snapped at it.

When he had the wire in his mouth, I let out some slack and the loop was big enough to wrap over his ears. His eyes rolled up and watched the noose go over his head. He didn't like it. He let go of the wire, and I flipped it under his jaw, then snapped the noose tight around his neck. I had him. He flopped and twisted like a fish on a hook, but I had locked the noose and there was no way he'd get far with the pole locked around his neck.

He shook his ears and twisted, then finally he calmed down. Dario and the woman officer came into the garage to help me, as the door opened and the owner came walking out. She flicked on the light, and for a second I felt so foolish standing there in her garage with her dog on the end of the pole. The Husky wagged his tail, and the tension in the pole slipped out as he moved toward the owner. I was surprised, and didn't know what to say. The owner was skinny but neat, with a ring on every long finger. She bent toward the dog, tears in her eyes, and I just held the pole on him.

"You bastard." She looked up at me, and then the Husky started to growl again. "Let him go you bastard. He's sick."

Her voice was shrill and crazy. Behind her another sheriff came through the door, reached down for her arm, thinking I had the dog under control, but his mouth was free. The Husky snapped. The cop flinched, a curse forming in his mouth, and the owner jumped at me. She was a small, fired-up woman, and she got the pole out of my hand somehow, screaming and pushing and kicking. I figured my job was to get the dog, so I just reached for his head. The woman was throwing punches into my chest and stomach, yelling about how they weren't going to get her. I wanted to get his mouth so he didn't bite anybody, but he was confused, trying to bite and protect his owner at the same time. I saw the panic in the dog's eyes as I broke past Dario and the sheriff and the skinny woman.

I got his head, but it was a weak grip, and he got out. I had to crush him to avoid getting bit. A dog bite took months to heal. I let myself fall on top of him, while holding my palms out where his face should be. The Husky fell to the floor. I crushed him under me while the owner fought the big sheriff who held her. He carried her back into the house, screaming at me and everybody, and she looked at Dario and pointed at him, then spit.

The Husky was slack beneath me. His eyes were glazed up and there was a sadness in them. I got off him, and he couldn't get up. He was lame in the right rear leg.

I carried the dog out of the garage to my truck. Dario followed and opened a cage on the truck. I placed the dog inside. Dario knew I was shook up. "It wasn't your fault," he said.

"What about the woman?"

Dario looked away, watching, I thought, the activity near the patrol cars. "What about her? She's upset. Said a Mexican broke into her house. When we get here, she's ballistic. Happens like that sometimes." He rubbed his neck and sighed heavy.

"I'm not sure what you mean, Dario. Did you catch him?"

"Who?"

"The Mexican."

"No. Supposed to be wearing a tan or a brown Stetson. Figure that? If you see him, give me a call anyway," Dario said and chuckled like he was joking.

"Anyway." I repeated. "I'm sure I broke that dog's leg."

Dario nodded and walked back to his patrol car with one hand raised in the air as if to say it was over. I drove the Husky back to Dr. Fielding's clinic.

* * *

The technician muzzled the dog, then flipped him on his side. Dr. Fielding was in his office watching some gameshow on the television. When he came out, he yawned and stretched, then took the dog's leg in his hands. Gently, he twisted the joint. The dog yelped, but the technician held him down.

"Femur's cracked." He yawned again, then rubbed the dog's nose and whispered to it.

It was good enough for a splint, a Bobby Jones as he called it. I was surprised the dog was so calm. He wrapped the Husky's leg in white, red, and blue tape. When he was done, he thumped it like a watermelon and smiled to himself.

"Don't come back today, Legget." He put his hands in his pockets and leaned against the treatment table.

"Are you serious? Don't know how many calls I might get today," I said as I signed the form.

"Yeah, think I'm going home. Need a drink or something."

"OK. Want me to take him?" I put my hand on the dog's neck.

Fielding looked at the dog. "No, I'll take care of him," he said and turned to the counter.

I caught him smiling in that strange way I'd seen him smile. I put the papers together and shut the notebook. Fielding was shaking his head and whispering to himself, kind of laughing. I didn't know what was going on.

"He needs rabies quarantine. Bit an officer."

"Animal Control?" He turned and asked.

"No, sheriff."

"Which one?"

"I don't know his name."

Fielding nodded and went back to work, the smile gone.

If Dr. Fielding wanted to keep the dog, that was OK. He knew Animal Control wouldn't pay him for any treatments beyond the splint he'd already put on. But the doc had done this before. Sometimes an animal just hit him a certain way and he kept it for nothing. I thought maybe this was one of those times.

* * *

I walked through the pound and saw Tom and Albert putting out food and water. I helped them finish up, then turned off the lights. I went up to John's office, but he wasn't there. I shut the door, dropped onto his couch and shut my eyes for a minute. The office smelled like pipe tobacco. I heard Molly Phelps in the next room, talking on the CB. The tobacco smell reminded me of the farm.

* * *

I had grown up on a farm, in a small house with an aluminum roof, and a porch made with warped scraps of lumber torn from a barn that had burned one summer. The porch was a faded green like the barn used to be. The house had three rooms and a kitchen. It had smelled like incense and cat piss. Stray cats had roamed the fields around it, on occasion making their ways inside. We ate beans and strawberries, when they were in season. I tracked the years not by the changing of the weather, but by strawberry pies, pudding, and whipped cream.

My mother had leased the house from Mrs. Dorothea Roy, who owned the farm, and hired migrant workers to pick strawberries. My mother was a half-Mexican migrant worker with bad ankles. They swelled up like ripe fruit, so she couldn't stoop and pick twelve hours a day. Two weeks into any month and all you heard was the shuffling of her feet and the groans she made with the effort of moving. By the end of the month, she couldn't walk and would sit by the window waiting for Dr. Diaz.

The doctor was a tall man with heavy round eyes and little scars in his cheeks, and dark hair. He moved like a boxer through the migrant workers who gathered around his black Mercedes once a month outside the picking shed. There were fights and babies and wounds from the combine to mend. Everyone knew Dr. Diaz worked for no pay.

My mother could see his car from where she sat. When he'd finally come, with dogs and sometimes a chicken at his heels, she'd blush and apologize for not getting up, and I could feel her lifting some. He'd split open that dark leather bag, draw a shot of milky fluid, give her the shot and say she'd be up in no time.

Then he would help her to the porch, set her down and fix his bag, sit next to her. I had listened to him talk. He twirled the end of his moustache and tapped his boot hard to make a point. By the time he was about to leave, my mother could walk. I never saw her pay him. But she thanked him with a word and a look like she'd move the whole house if she could, just to get it out of his way. She told me later he was the only man she'd ever trusted.

Sometimes he'd given me a dollar to bring his car around. Driving it just that short way gave me status with the workers. They must have thought I was related, and surely it had saved me from some fights. I lingered with the keys and drove it slow to keep down dust. The other boys lined up and watched.

I remembered waiting on the porch with Dr. Diaz for a coroner. When she'd died I was seventeen. He'd tried to show me how to hand roll a cigarette while we sat there waiting, then asked me what I knew about town.

"What do you want to do, Coleman?" he'd asked. He was the last person I could remember who'd used my first name.

Maybe my memory had failed me, or my dream of going back had taken over my senses, but I could catch only glimpses of my early life, like faded photographs, images that seemed to come from nowhere and correlate with nothing. Public school, stray dogs, fields of strawberries, and furrowed dirt. I didn't care about going back to Mrs. Dorothea Roy's farm. What I wanted was to go back to something like it. Someplace with the same slow mornings, and lots of green. I remember telling my mother that I wanted to have fifty dogs on a ranch in the mountains, maybe, but I had never seen mountains, just read about them, imagined them. She had smiled and touched the back of my head. I still felt the strange tingle her old hand made against my neck, where the first whiskers grew.

The phone rang. I raised myself from the couch and saw it was after four. I walked to the bathroom. I heard Tom and Albert in the back, in the kennel, their hoses splashing against the cement walls. Molly Phelps came out of her office, a spill of red hair over her left shoulder, makeup caked on her face.

"Legget, what are you doing here? I've been trying to call you for an hour. John's looking for you." She dropped her purse on the counter like an exclamation.

"Sorry, I must have dozed off."

"There's some trouble with the Holton case."

"Who?" Sleep had slowed me.

"The Husky that bit the sheriff today." She touched her lip. "Holton's her name."

"Can you hold on a second?" I went into the bathroom and threw cold water on my face. Trouble. And I had to hear it from Molly Phelps.

When I returned, she said, "Are you ready for this Legget? Did you know she caught someone breaking in? My god, this town is getting just like Miami."

"I was there; that's what they said."

"Well, Ms. Holton was taken to the hospital. I'm not sure why. Hysterics, maybe. That's what John told me. He said she's tickled spitless. Now, what does that mean? I think it means she's OK. What do you think, Legget?"

"I've seen worse." I leaned some weight on my other leg. "But what's the problem?"

"Ms. Holton's raising hell with the sheriff's department and Animal Control. Apparently, she's got a cousin or a boyfriend or God knows what in the courthouse, because John thinks it's a pretty serious situation. He said he'd like to give that bitch a combing out. You know John's mad when he starts talking like that. You know what I mean, Legget? Want a Coke?" She smiled and picked up her purse.

"No, but thanks Molly. I better call John."

"Just wait for him here." She waved good-bye, showing off her long, red fingernails, and left by the front door.

I went back to John's office. If John was anything he was loyal to his employees. I didn't have to fear him taking this out on me. But somebody might get spooked.

The media loved to get hold of us. Sometimes they paid us some respect and did a short piece for the late news about how hard we worked at the pound. They'd tote their cameras into the kennel and get some good shots of the puppies and kittens, then talk about our adoption service. It created a little rush for about two weeks, but there were problems with the positive coverage too. Last time they'd shot film in the kennel, it was one week before Christmas. During the holidays we shut down the adoption service because people would adopt animals, then give them to people who didn't really want them. A week or so later we'd get them back. So John had nipped the problem in the bud, by saying: No adoptions, at all, during any holidays.

Then there was the time that someone at Channel 62 had heard a rumor that there was an outbreak of parvo in our kennel. Parvovirus was an airborne disease that dogs caught. It attacked their intestines which, for weeks, shot bloody diarrhea. If a dog caught parvo, he died. The antibiotics and IV fluids were too costly for Animal Control, and considering the fact that the animal would most likely die anyway, we put them to sleep. The Parvo bug swept through the kennel in a matter of days. We had twenty to thirty sick dogs at a time. We hauled at least ten a day to vets to be put to sleep. Then, when the daily death toll increased to twenty, we called the vets to the kennel.

ACOs kept bringing dogs in from the streets. The new dogs caught the bug. An epidemic could set us back for months. We stopped the adoption service. We hired veterinary technicians to supervise. That was when Channel 62 caught on. It may have been the outside help we got from the techs, or the many times John had to go the city manager for more money, but they showed up one afternoon when we were piling dogs in the incinerator and filmed it, live at five. On the streets, after the telecast, kids threw rocks at our trucks. Drivers cut us off and even tried to run us off the road. How could we explain? We had no control over incurable diseases. And what were we going to do with all the animals?

I had been at Animal Control for about two years when the parvo epidemic struck, and I was unprepared. Nobody had said it could happen, and nobody had told me what it would be like. John had called me off the streets. I spent eight hours a day spraying bloody diarrhea off the walls of the kennel, off the backs of the dogs, off the floor. I carried warm, wet bodies from the kennel to the incinerator, five six, seven times a day. The smokestack of the incinerator spit fumes for thirty-six hours straight. I wore a surgical mask to keep from retching at the powerfully sweet smell of digested blood.

After two days, I couldn't take it. I went to John, and slammed my fist on his desk. He looked up slowly, fixed the papers I had knocked out of order, and motioned me to a seat. He told me I had a right to be mad. He told me I wouldn't be there if I didn't love the animals, if I didn't care about them. And since I cared, I had to do what needed to be done to save the healthy ones. He had told me the epidemic was like a war.

That was the first time John and I went to Greenhorns. He bought me lunch, though I had a hard time eating. He told me I needed to make up for things in other ways. I needed to care about every animal that I caught on the streets in a way that reminded me of how bad it could really be.

* * *

It didn't seem like John was coming back to his office so I called his house and talked to Beth, who said he was on his way. He had been at the courthouse all afternoon. She told me to come over for supper, and I agreed.

Beth had been an English teacher in public school and met John when he'd toured there, giving lectures on the importance of rabies vaccines. I enjoyed talking with Beth. Sometimes John and I skated around a subject, then eventually stumbled onto the truth. But with Beth, I just said whatever was on my mind. I liked her for that.

John and Beth lived in an apartment complex on Kelly Road, near Saint Alfred's Church and a private school that she claimed was the best in the state if you had the money. When I parked beneath their second-floor apartment, I didn't notice John's truck and was glad he wasn't there. I'd have a chance to talk with Beth before I saw him.

The door was open, and I smelled green beans and bacon on the stove. I wiped my boots on the mat and walked inside.

"Beth?" I heard her moving pots in the kitchen sink just around the corner.

Their apartment was decorated with brass teapots displayed on a walnut-stained coffee table, beneath brownish wallpaper with pictures of pumpkins, apples, and milk jugs. A Siamese cat named Dozer lounged on the couch. He looked up when I came in, flicked his tail, then went back to sleep.

Beth came out of the kitchen wiping her hands on a faded blue apron she wore around the apartment. She had said it hid her fat as well as anything. But she was a sweet woman, and it was easy to see why John loved her. Her light, wiry hair was tied in a ponytail, but it was frizzed and stuck out like she had been electrocuted. She smiled and waved me in.

"Well, hello, Legget." She pulled me over to the couch. "Want something to drink?"

"Scotch?"

"Nope. I threw it out last Wednesday. John's not sleeping well, and he thinks a glass of scotch helps." She turned off the television.

"It probably does put him to sleep." I sat on the couch.

"Of course it does, but at what cost? I got tea, milk, and water."

"Anything."

"God, I hate when people say that. What the hell do you *want* to drink?"

"Water."

"Thank you."

She brought me a glass of iced water and sat on a high-backed wicker chair facing the door. Dozer jumped into her lap and purred.

"John should be here soon." She stroked the cat.

"Did he call?"

"Yes. He told me about it. Don't worry. He knows it's not your fault. The woman's just blowing smoke to stay out of trouble."

I nodded but didn't really believe it. I heard his boots on the stairs.

Beth stared out the open door. "John's here."

He walked in with a brown paper bag under his arm. Beth stood and they hugged each other in the open door. John slapped my arm, set the bag on the counter, then walked into the back.

"Let me change my clothes," he said over his shoulder.

Beth went to the kitchen. When John came out with jeans and a bare chest, Beth served up dinner. John opened the bottle of scotch, and we had a small glass.

"So tell me what happened," John said with a fork full of beans an inch from his mouth. I pushed away from the table, my plate half-empty, and told him what had happened after I left him in Greenhorns. He listened closely and nodded.

"Well, I knew you were all right, Legget. I just need to know the facts so I can deal with the shitheads at City Hall. You know that. Anyway, Ms. Holton's after us and the sheriff's department. She said you provoked her dog, and then beat on it with the rabies pole. Normally, it wouldn't mean shit, but the lady has some friends who are interested in her welfare."

"What are they going to do?"

Beth patted my hand. John shrugged. "Probably nothing. But they want an investigation. They're sending someone tomorrow or the next day. I'm sorry, Legget. You were in the wrong place at the wrong time. The county moves slower than a dead man on crutches. Maybe they'll run out of steam before things get out of hand."

"You're not going to suspend me?" If John suspended me, I'd lose the body tour, and a lot of money.

"Of course not." Then John was quiet a minute. Beth stopped eating. Her fork tinked against the plate. John said, "But it wouldn't hurt to be careful."

"Be careful? What does that mean?"

"Come off the streets. A few days maybe. Just till things cool down."

Chapter 3

I helped Albert and Tom clean in the morning, and I was sure I bugged the hell out of them because I was full of energy and good intentions.

I discovered a blue tick hound in one of the cages. He'd been brought in a few days ago by another dog catcher from Lawton Kennel on the north side of Sawyer Road. The owners had left the dog to be boarded while they went to Canada, but never returned. The Sawyer Road kennel kept the hound two weeks later than the deposit would hold him, then called us.

I took him into the field by the incinerator during lunch and ran with him on a leash at first, but the dog seemed so glad to have someone with him, I took the leash off his neck, and he stayed next to me without a problem. I let him root through the bushes and dig holes under the fence. Pretty soon he had developed a distance that he felt comfortable with. He'd move about thirty feet away from me while glancing back to make sure I wouldn't leave him. His owners had called him Cal. He was a year old, with a shiny coat which surprised me. Three weeks in a boarding kennel and a couple in ours would cut the shine from a dog's coat and eyes as sure as anything.

But Cal was young, and full of energy. I needed that kind of energy to keep my head above the waters that seemed to be getting just a little deeper. Cal got me to thinking about my farm, and how right it would have been to take the hound and let him live there. We had to hold him another five days before putting him up for adoption, and I knew he wouldn't last. The first person who saw him behind the rusty cage wires would take him because he was purebred. His coat was thick, with patches of brown over his back. His ears flopped down past his jaw, and his teeth were white as angels' wings.

I got him to bark by teasing him with a tennis ball I found in the grass, and he made a lot of noise. I'd have heard his bark at night in the deadest sleep of the week and known there was something wrong. A good dog.

I spent an extra hour of my lunch with Cal in the field. John wasn't loaded with things for me to do, and Tom and Albert had enough bosses without me trailing their heels. I remembered when I had worked the kennel and how much I hated being thrown off my routine. I played with Cal till he dropped by my boots with a snort and closed his eyes. Only a dog could sleep in the afternoon sun, and Cal had decided it was time for a nap. I lay on the grass next to him and propped my head against his chest. He let me stay until the ants found us and we had to go back inside.

Cal didn't want to go back into the cage, and he started to whimper when I opened the gate. I went in and coaxed him to lay down on the plastic rack that kept him off the cold cement floor. He finally did it, and I brought him an extra bowl of food. I petted him again through the closed cage door and wished I didn't have to leave him. Dogs were sometimes better than people.

I went to John's office. I heard him yell to Molly in an impatient voice before I saw his half-closed door. I pushed it open and smelled the remains of lunch. Seafood, something. Molly Phelps was in the next room. I felt the cold from her air conditioning seeping under the door. It felt good, and John was in a good mood, which wasn't exactly how I had wanted him that morning, but then I was glad.

"Mr. Leland." I walked in.

"Hello." He clenched his pipe in his teeth.

I sat on the couch and noticed a new picture of Beth on his desk. I looked at it and felt, for a moment, that I was a part of their family. We were one family, and I liked that feeling. They had made me feel wanted from the very start. Right then I appreciated John being in charge of things. I liked the slow, careful way he ran the kennel. I liked the order of his desk and office. It made me feel like he knew exactly what he was doing there. But I knew the streets were different.

"Do you remember that blue tick that came from Lawton Kennel?" I tapped the desk.

"Yep." John flipped open a small box filled with index cards. "Cal. Eleven months old. Got all his vaccines. He's got five days, and he won't last one when he's up for adoption. The owner owes Lawton Kennel some money."

Sometimes, if a dog came to Animal Control from a veterinarian or a kennel, it came with a price tag. An old trick was to bring your dog to a vet for the treatment of an illness or boarding and not pay the bill. Eventually, the vet would send the dog to us, and then the owner would come adopt him for twelve dollars. They saved hundreds from the unpaid vet bill. The only way we could stop them was to get ID from the adopting family and check it against the records from the vet or the kennel. If it happened, we made the debtor return to the place the dog came from and settle up.

"I want him."

"Oh, yeah?" John was surprised because he knew I was saving money for a place of my own. He had even clipped advertisements from the Sunday papers and brought them to me on Monday mornings. I had thanked him, slipped the clippings in my front pocket and told him I just wasn't ready.

"What are you waiting for?" he had asked.

I had told him I didn't know, money maybe, but inside I knew differently. I was waiting for a sign, for things to fall into place naturally. I was the kind who rolled with the punches. I grabbed at opportunity like a fish darted for bait. I didn't know if it was the best way to live a life, but it was comfortable. I'd got pretty far off of lucky rolls, but the body tour was luck, and it was making me a down payment. I would know when I was ready, when it was time to strike.

"What do I have to do?"

"Wait," John said, and smiled. "I'd take him myself if Beth would let me have a dog, but she won't. Besides, you don't know if he's flawed yet."

"I know."

The problem with dogs that came to the pound was this: you couldn't tell what kind of life they'd had before then. Most of them had some flaw, like pissing on the floor when the doorbell rang or a mortal fear of bearded men in hats. Maybe that dog would freeze up when something scared it. Maybe it wouldn't bark if someone tried to break into the trailer. You just never knew until that thing happened, and there it was.

The next day was Thursday, and first thing in the morning I was with Cal in the back field by the incinerator. I didn't care so much about his flaws. I thought I could fix them if he had any. The grass at the bottom of the fence was lush and soft because no one ever walked near it, and the dogs always pissed there when they were allowed out, which wasn't often, but enough over the years to fertilize the grass. It was one of the things I had never noticed till Cal ran off to dig near the bushes. With my fingers I felt how soft the grass was, and right then I knew why it had grown so well. It struck me with such a fondness for the kennel and being outside and enjoying the warm sun that I instantly thought of the farm again. The idea of the farm, and for a few moments I was lost in a kind of daze, and imagined I was there, and Cal was really my dog, and he was off chasing rabbits.

Cal was chasing something. I heard him bark. I'd never heard him bark in fear or anger, but somehow I knew what it would sound like. Of course it would be different than his shrill, rumbling bark I heard now. John stepped out of the building and yelled my name twice before I realized he was after me. I called Cal, and he charged back, but stopped when he saw that I was heading back to the cages. I coaxed him with a friendly call; his ears perked up, and then he ran to me. I locked him up, patted him a few times on the head, and told John about the grass. He just looked at me and raised his eyebrows. He was in such a different frame of mind, I realized he had no idea what I meant, really, and so I dropped the topic.

"What's up?"

"I'll show you." He headed toward his office.

His radio was off, and Molly must have been at lunch because I didn't hear the CB static, and John had the phone propped up on a few hardback books. He put his scuffed, black loafers on the desk and leaned back in his chair.

"I got a good one for you. Took the call while you were out playing mountain man." John struck a match and touched the flame to the bowl of his pipe. The pipe bubbled and released a cloud of thick, black smoke. It smelled like burning wood.

I waved my hand in front of my face. "Jesus, what is that?"

"Cavendish. Do you know Julius Gant?"

"The veterinarian?"

"He called and filed a complaint. An official complaint, and that's strange. He said a letter's coming in the mail."

"What's his problem?" I asked.

"Greyhounds," John said, and blew the hideous smoke into the air.

They were back. It was that time of the year when the greyhound people drove their dilapidated trucks around town. They hung out in cheap restaurants, motels, old buildings, and the track.

Palm County's track was built lopsided, and the grass in the winner's circle had always been brown no matter how hard the landscapers tried to grow it. You could tell the track was lopsided when you were sitting in the stands. You had this feeling that the earth was rotating to the left, and you were going along with it. When the track was open, there were usually two or three slip-and-fall injuries in the stands.

Many veterinarians disliked the greyhound people because they were notorious for unpaid bills, petty lawsuits, and sometimes a malicious vandalization of hospital grounds. Veterinarians fresh from school, eager to get a practice off its feet, saw greyhound clients in hopes that they could establish a steady flow of cash, be it ever so small. There was no such thing as insurance for dogs, at least not any that was worth paying for, and so the vets needed money that came straight out of pocket.

John showed me his notes. "Gant claimed that Diamond Kennel is using steroids on their dogs. I told him we needed evidence, and he said they were buying boxes, not a bottle of pills, but a box of bottles. I guess that makes for evidence?"

"How does he know?"

"Wouldn't say. I want you to go down there and look it over. Wear your civvies and take the body truck."

"He should call the Greyhound Association or the AVMA."

"I know, but Gant's a good fella. He's helped out with wildlife. You know that, Legget. Besides, we got to cover our ass."

Dog catchers not only patrolled the streets, but we investigated cases involving animal cruelty, vicious animals, and health hazards. It didn't surprise me that the greyhounders were feeding steroids to the racers. They gave it to the pups so they would grow bigger and faster than they would on horsemeat and rabbit blood. I supposed they thought it couldn't hurt to make a good dog better. It meant more money, and the risks of getting caught were low. It was simple. Testosterone made the pups grow bigger faster, and epinephrine was used just before a race to make their hearts pound harder.

Most of the trainers had a special veterinarian they went to. The vet unloaded large quantities of blue liniment, penicillin, Strongid T (for hookworm), and that meant money. The trainers got advice, an account, and whatever medicine they needed.

I drove home to my trailer and changed into jeans and an old Polo shirt with holes in the back and under the arms. I ate a fried-egg sandwich in the kitchen, copied the directions to the Diamond Kennel on a clean sheet of paper, and tucked it in my back pocket. I knew a little about the dogs. It had been a topic of interest to me when I first started work for Animal Control. I had gone to the public library and asked the only librarian in the place to help me find some books.

The greatest racing greyhound that had ever lived was Mick the Miller. He had been owned by an Irish priest back in the late 1920s. Mick the Miller had won every race he entered in Ireland, then made his way to London, where he did the same. The priest agreed to sell Mick to a London trainer for four thousand pounds and the purse if the dog won the derby. Mick the Miller was a brindle, sixty-six pounds, as quick as a bullet, and he won the derby.

Mick the Miller, Never Roll, Lucky Pilot, Jolly Irishman were greyhound legends of the sport's past. And in the past, maybe like all things, an illusion of something better obscured the doping and the watering of the dogs before races, the horsemeat, and the cramped cages, but regardless, things were not the same.

Greyhounders committed a variety of crimes that no one seemed to notice, especially the State. Animal Control didn't have the time or the authority to police the racing circuit. It was supposed to be the job of the International Greyhound Association. What we could do was bust the owners on animal cruelty charges, but they wouldn't always stick. It was up to a judge to decide.

* * *

Maulbron highway was about twenty-five miles long. It twisted past shopping malls, pawn shops, car dealers, convenience stores, offices, and traffic. I noticed how the town was spreading out little by little. That particular slice of Maulbron was not the area I normally patrolled.

The businesses started to thin out. I saw more housing developments, then shacks, and long stretches of saw grass and palm hummocks. Dead shrub filled with road dust and rats.

The city changed into suburb, and then into something else. I didn't know what to call it. The outskirts of town? But whatever it was called, it was the right place for a kennel. The greyhounders liked to be away from the flow, and they needed cheap space.

I found the Sawyer Road sign. I started to sweat; the sun was just heating up. Sawyer Road was narrow, and I turned onto it slowly.

About halfway down the road, I saw a rusty, metal sign that said Diamond Kennels. It ran above a two-post, wooden fence that trailed a quarter mile along the length of a well-used gravel road. I stopped the truck in front of the road and looked down. I didn't see anything but a few rickety, white buildings at the other end. I honked the horn a few times. Nobody answered, of course, but I was nervous.

I unwrapped a package of Sweets and lit one with the truck lighter. I smoked for a second, then backed up, pulled the truck into the gravel road, and gunned down it. My truck raised huge, white clouds of dust as I watched the buildings come into view. I hoped someone there would see or hear my truck coming down the path so I didn't surprise any men with shotguns. It wouldn't be the first time an Animal Control officer had been met with a frown and a two-barrel.

The buildings looked like old Army barracks. One building faced the other in the shape of an L. In between the buildings the chain link fencing sparkled in the sunlight. The fences were a sure sign that I was in the right place, and when I turned the corner at a slow crawl, I saw a beat-up red truck with the ventilated greyhound cages on top of the bed. The passenger door of the truck had once showed Diamond's name, but now it said MOND KENN L. Next to the red truck was a blue Toyota Camry with a long CB antennae and fancy, chrome mags. I parked next to the red truck and honked once more.

I saw two men standing in between the cages. The one facing me wore cut-off jeans and rubber sandals. He had a crop of red hair flopped over to one side and a red beard. He wore dark wraparound sunglasses and a faded T-shirt. The other man had his back to me, but I could see he was tall and thin, with grey curly hair and old hiking boots. When I slammed the truck door, the tall man turned around, and I noticed right away the horn-rimmed glasses and the long nose, the receding hairline over the jewel-green eyes. Dr. Fielding.

At first I was surprised. I had expected greyhounders, not Dr. Fielding. But then I realized he might have been up there on a call for a sick dog, and if that was true, it was a good sign. If Diamond Kennels cared enough about their dogs to pay a vet to come down at two in the afternoon, then they couldn't be all that bad.

I waved and shouted, "Hey, Doc!"

Dr. Fielding turned back to the red-haired man, said something, then helped him lift a cardboard box. The red-haired man carried the box into the building, and Dr. Fielding turned around.

"Legget," he said, "what the hell are you doing here?" He pushed up his sleeves and extended his large hand.

"A little business," I said.

He stood in the middle of the path that led through the outside runs. His hands were in his pockets, then running through his hair. All at once I was aware of the cigar burning the tips of my fingers. I shook my hand like a wasp had stung it, and the cigar sparked on the gravel. Dr. Fielding took my hand and looked at the burn.

"Second degree. Come on."

I followed him to the side of the building where he bent over with a pocket knife and cut a stem from an aloe plant. Aloe plants grew along the length of the building like weeds.

"Let's see your hand." He reached out for it.

"It's not that bad, Doc. I've got work to do."

He squeezed the syrup from the piece of aloe, and rubbed it between my fingers. "This is an awkward situation." He tossed the stem against the side of the building.

"What are you doing here, Doc?"

"Business. Just like you. I'm in the box at the track tonight." His pocket knife snapped when the blade went back into the sheath. He slipped the knife into his pocket.

The box was a room at the dog track where a veterinarian stayed during the night's races to attend any injured animals, inspect their paws, and confirm that the animals were in good health before they raced. It was required by law. Actually, the vet never really checked the animals beforehand. There were too many of them and not enough time. It was an unwritten rule that the vet just okayed the hounds without looking at them. If a vet raised a fuss about the slack procedures, he wasn't invited back.

"What's the big deal? I've got some work to do. You've got nothing to do with it. Right?"

"That's right, Legget." He put his arm around my shoulders, and we walked back to the cluster of cages.

The red-haired man was inside a cage taunting a young greyhound with a white towel. The hound grabbed the towel in his teeth and shook. The man growled and punched the dog lightly in the shoulders. He looked up when we turned the corner.

"Hey, Sam," Dr. Fielding said, "this is Legget. He's a friend of mine, and he'd like to see the kennel."

Sam stepped out of the cage. He removed his sunglasses. His eyes were black. I'd never seen eyes like them before. I didn't think it was possible for eyes to be that dark. When I got closer, I saw he had drops of spit in his beard.

"I'm from Animal Control."

Sam's black eyes opened and let the light in. They beamed like two small pieces of heated charcoal. His jaw finally closed. He looked at Dr. Fielding, who was a head taller than either of us, and Dr. Fielding nodded.

"OK," Sam said. His mouth hardly opened. "Cathy can show you the place." He pointed to a pair of open doors about twenty feet away, at the tail end of the first building.

I walked straight ahead, not looking back. I didn't want to see Dr. Fielding's face. I didn't want to find anything wrong, but I had to check the place out.

I felt rivulets of sweat race down my back and soak into my jeans. I sensed the woman inside the building but didn't see her.

"Cathy?" I took a step closer.

"Yes?" Her voice rose, then broke off.

I stepped into the building.

"We've got tin roofs," she said as if explaining the heat. She had brown hair in a ponytail that reached her waist, wore dark nylon shorts and a bathing-suit top. A leather bandana was wrapped around her forehead. No makeup, she was a rough, hewn woman with bumps and light blonde hair on her arms and legs. A box fan pushed the air around.

"I'm Cathy. " She extended her hand. A sterling silver bracelet had a chunk of turquoise set in.

She was chopping lettuce on the counter with a butcher knife. Behind her, there was a stack of wire cages with white and brown rabbits inside. She finished chopping the lettuce and dumped it in a ceramic bowl. I stepped closer to pick up a piece that had fallen to the floor.

She carried the bowl to the cages, then stuffed the lettuce through the circles in the wire.

"Are they pets?" I asked, even though I knew they were for training.

"Actually they are." She lifted her chin.

"I need to look around a little," I offered.

"I guess I can't stop you," she said.

She turned for more lettuce. I grabbed the ceramic bowl, then handed it to her. "Sam told me you could help."

"Sam." She said the name to herself.

"He said you could help." I took the empty bowl from her hands.

I noticed Sam on the other side of the complex, eyeing us suspiciously. But when Sam disappeared, Cathy relaxed. I was easy with her and tried to show the right amount of respect for her work and knowledge of the dogs.

She showed me Jelly Roll, Acme, Diamond Jim Dandy, Torpedo Joe, The Slider. They nudged their cages when Cathy walked by. Each one had a special bark, or a weak leg, a tendency to roll while racing, a fear of noise, or maybe, a talent for speed, and she knew every one. I didn't see anything out of line. The cages were clean and roomy, much nicer than other kennels I had seen that were dirty and cramped. No special touches, but she seemed to be a different kind of trainer. She knew her dogs well and seemed to care about them. I didn't quite understand how she was connected with Sam and Dr. Fielding. She was there. She must have known something about doping, about watering, about overfeeding before a race so the dog would run slow, but I didn't want to ask her, at least not then.

After we toured the kennel, she took me to the office. As we approached I heard Dr. Fielding's voice from inside. The office was cramped and stale, like an office in the back of an auto repair shop. Dr. Fielding sat on a stool facing an aluminum desk that Sam was behind. Sam twirled a spoon in his hand and laughed at something Cathy and I had missed. They stopped when we crammed ourselves into the small room, closing the door so the air conditioning wouldn't seep out.

"What do you think, Legget? Nice kennel or what?" Dr. Fielding asked.

Sam got up, pulled a Coke from a small refrigerator behind the desk.

"Want one?" He looked at Cathy.

Cathy turned to me, smiled, and asked if I wanted a Coke. I shook my head, but Dr. Fielding took one, then pulled a folding chair from behind a stuffed file cabinet. He split the chair open and offered it to Cathy. She sat down, and I looked down at her chest; I couldn't resist. I saw where her skin turned pale.

Sam stared at me. "Going to shut the place down?"

"I didn't see anything wrong. You got a nice kennel."

"Then what are you doing? Just a friendly visit?" He slammed the Coke can on the desk.

Cathy stood, cleaned the spilled Coke from the desk, and gave Sam a dirty look.

"My brother's a real jerk. Don't you think?"

Dr. Fielding laughed. "Look, we all got to get along."

I agreed.

Dr. Fielding looked at Sam. "Why don't you tell us why you're here, Legget. That'll be a good start."

At first I thought I should lie, but they all knew I wouldn't have come to the kennel unless there was a specific reason. They knew Animal Control did not police the trainers, at least not as a matter of routine. I looked at Cathy. She waited for me to answer, her arms folded across her chest. The blue bathing-suit top strained around her shoulders.

"There was a complaint. Someone's concerned about your dogs getting doped."

"OK," Dr. Fielding said. "That's good." He sat on the folding chair, between me and the desk. "So, Legget. What would you do if you found, say, some kind of dope?"

"I'd want to see a prescription from a veterinarian."

"Which I am. Correct?" Dr. Fielding raised his Coke in the air and laughed a forced laugh. He was smiling. The room was quiet except for the breathing and the air conditioner.

"Perfect," Sam said.

Cathy walked around the desk, and opened a drawer. She took out a white, manila envelope and handed it to Dr. Fielding. He opened it, and I saw a wad of cash inside. Dr. Fielding counted the money in his huge hands.

"Legget likes to play the dogs. Hell, I know that." He said.

Sam stood up, grunted, and left the office. Cathy sat in his chair behind the desk.

"He's suspicious of everyone," she said. "He likes the dogs more than people."

"He's a fucking asshole." I shook my head. I felt a whole lot better without Sam in the room. I could trust the doctor, and I believed I could trust Cathy some.

"Does he know about body tour, Doc?"

"Of course not. That's between us." He took a bundle of the money, and put the rest in the envelope. He gave the envelope to Cathy. She slipped it back into the drawer.

"Want to go to the races tonight?" Dr. Fielding smiled, then laughed.

"Sure," I said, then looked at Cathy.

* * *

Dr. Fielding had asked me to bet seventy-five dollars on Torpedo Joe in the third race, to win. I took the money because I trusted him. I liked him, too. He was an old boy. John trusted him. I followed Cathy back to the shed where the rabbits were caged. She finished passing out the shreds of lettuce. I guessed my day there was over. I had hoped something would happen with Cathy, and I supposed it had in a way. Sam was gone, Dr. Fielding was off to the track with him, and I was alone with her.

"Do you need a ride to the track?" I asked. I knew I needed to check in with John. I was in civilian clothes and had an unmarked truck. Perfect. I could call John on the mobile and see him the next day.

Cathy didn't answer. I said, "I don't have an air conditioner, but it'll be cool later ..."

"I hate air conditioning."

"Great. So, do you need a ride?"

"Not really," she said almost in a whisper.

"Do you want a ride?"

"Sure."

I was catching on.

She finished up the rabbits, then walked through the kennel checking locks and gates. She made sure the dogs had water. Diamond Kennel had fourteen dogs. That wasn't many, but it was a tidy number. You could easily take care of fourteen healthy dogs. At our kennel, it was impossible to take care of so many animals, many of them with mange, upper respiratory infections, ear mites, hookworm, and fleas. At that point, it was easy to justify the fact that I had seventy-five dollars in my pocket, and I was already mentally listing the good things I'd tell John about Diamond Kennels.

Chapter 4

She had changed into a dress with a black checkerboard pattern across the hem, the middle, and the sleeves. It was tight around her waist. She had bright freckles on her neck and shoulders, and a good tan. Her hair was loose and long, falling down her back and shining.

I parked my truck around the corner of the large building where Cathy pointed. There were twelve or fifteen greyhound trucks parked there also. Some of the greyhounders stood by their trucks smoking and talking. They looked at us, but didn't seem to care. We went through a door near the trucks and through a long hallway with gray fuse boxes and fluorescent lights hanging from a high ceiling. Up two flights of cement stairs to a booth above the racing track. The booth was like a wedge above the bleachers.

The booth was long and narrow and filled with people. They wore suits and dresses. There was a bar in the corner and betting booths at the far end. Televisions were bolted above the glass windows that faced the track below. I bought two beers.

"What is this place?" I touched Cathy's back.

She whispered, "I think these people just took a contract to rebuild the track, update it a little."

The track was old and small. It wasn't anything like tracks in

Miami or Tampa. Palm County was much smaller, and the greyhound people stayed only two weeks out of the year.

Cathy leaned against the glass with a pair of binoculars. A tractor pulling a steel rake combed out the dirt. About half of the bleachers beneath us were filled.

"Do you watch from here every night?" I dropped my leg over the back of a chair.

"No, I'm usually downstairs, but I knew we could sneak in here tonight."

I held up my form. "Who should I bet on?"

"You know that already."

People lined up at the betting booth, counted out a few one-dollar bills as they rubbed their hands over their ironed shirts. Even if they picked a winner, they'd earn just a few dollars, then bet the winnings again. Maybe, an even-odds dog, to win, place or show. I had known a few old-time dog gamblers. Harley Wilcox, who pumped gas at the Shell Station, Pearl Boyer, Palm County's bingo queen, who swallowed a handful of tranquilizers just after her cat died. Both had told me never to go there with more than fifty dollars in your pockets. The horses were the real money. The horses were the big time.

"Legget." Cathy touched my shoulder. "Do you want to bet on the first race?"

"Are any of your dogs in it?"

"No."

"I'll wait."

The trainers walked their dogs across the first stretch, displaying the colored blankets draped across their backs. The announcer introduced the dog, the trainer, the kennel, the owner. The greyhounds were silver, black, brown, brindle, and white. The dogs looked like children on the track.

Cathy tapped my shoulder and pointed. "That's Blue Thunder."

The trainer holding the dog was a pudgy, long-haired man with dark sunglasses and a deep tan. Cathy told me that Blue Thunder was the fastest dog on the tracks that year, but he was in the class above the Diamond dogs, and they would not have to face him till next season. Blue Thunder was the favorite in the first race. The dogs were lined into the chutes as the people in the booth surged closer to the windows and the televisions.

The rabbit shot from the fence. The dogs popped from their chutes a moment later, chasing it like fiends. In a second, the dogs turned the corner. Cathy watched them through her binoculars, while the others in the booth yelled and laughed, cheering their bets to win.

I could barely see the dogs on the other side. They were one pack that moved across the brown turf. My palms itched. I wished I had bet on the first race. Cathy could have told me to bet on Blue Thunder. I wondered why she hadn't. Did she think it was wrong? I didn't understand these people. I could have looked on the form and seen that Blue Thunder was the favorite. I could have read his statistics for myself and decided he was sure to win. Maybe I should have just asked.

Around the last turn the dogs came into view. Blue Thunder was in the lead, a good four lengths ahead of the pack. A black hound was second, and the rest of the pack was clustered behind them. Before Blue Thunder reached the finish line, Cathy handed me the binoculars, and I watched him cross. The black box swallowed the rabbit, and the dogs slowed. The trainers burst from the sidelines and fetched their dogs before a fight could break out.

"He's fast." She pulled her hair back.

"Can your dogs beat him?" I gave her the binoculars.

Cathy lifted the warm beer to her lips, then set it down without drinking.

"Do you want another one?"

"No, thanks. We could probably beat him, but our dogs aren't Class A yet. We'll see how they do."

"Is Blue Thunder drugged?"

"What do you mean?"

"Is Blue Thunder doped before he races?" I swallowed the last of my beer.

"How would I know? It happens. I don't know." She turned to the track. Two workers raked up the dirt around the starting gate, in preparation for the next race.

A woman standing close to us spilled her drink on the window ledge and laughed. A busboy rushed over and cleaned it up. She held out her hand, and the glass was replaced with a fresh drink, a wedge of lime stabbed on the rim.

Cathy wasn't going to tell me anything, and I wasn't sure I wanted to push her hard enough to find out. What did it matter to me? I wanted Cathy more than I wanted to close the kennel. There were more reasons to leave it alone than not to.

I walked to the bar and ordered a ginger ale, wishing the night was over. I went to the betting table and tossed the seventy-five to the man behind the computer. He wasn't impressed. He looked at me and kind of laughed behind his moustache. He knew I was poor, that I was nobody. I dug thirty more out of my own pocket and bought another ticket to win, third race, just like Fielding had told me. Cathy smiled as I walked back with the tickets and drink in my hand. I handed her the doctor's ticket. She shook her head and told me it wasn't hers.

"I'm not allowed to bet."

"Neither is Dr. Fielding." I looked around to make sure no one was listening, but realized no one cared what we were doing. They were drinking, losing money. They weren't real gamblers. The real gamblers owned the dogs. Real gamblers went to Vegas or someplace. Riverboats, maybe. Did they still have riverboats? I wondered. The real gamblers might have cared, or maybe they would have just laughed.

I watched Sam walk onto the dirt with Torpedo Joe. The dog wore a red blanket with black and white diamonds. The dog was jumpy. He lunged against the leash and trotted. A man standing next to me commented on Joe's enthusiasm, bummed a few dollars from the woman with him, and went off to bet. Cathy watched Sam through the binoculars.

"He looks anxious."

"It's only his third race." She watched the other dogs walk the dirt. "That's Lacey Lady. Sam and I used to work for the owner. Curry's their name. They wouldn't let Sam train the dogs the way we thought they needed to be trained. They're slow, you'll see."

"How much will we win?" I leaned closer to her. She turned from the binoculars, but still held them up. Her face was inches from mine.

"I don't know, a few hundred maybe. Joe's got long odds because he didn't place in his second race. He came in fourth the first time on the track. I think he was distracted by all the noise and lights. I didn't want him to race at night, but we make more money."

"How long has Sam been doing this?"

"About ten years. We grew up on the dogs, horses, baseball games."

We waited for the gun. Torpedo Joe had to run only one quarter of a mile to win.

"He hates the box." Cathy said. "I left him in the carrier three nights in a row, but he still hates it."

The rabbit jumped off the gate again, and the dogs went after it. Cathy perched closer to the window and keyed on Joe. I knew she was watching for any strange movements, watching his eyes above the wire and plastic muzzle. Torpedo Joe broke in front easily. He was a good two lengths ahead of Lacey Lady.

"I thought you said she was slow."

"Shut up," she muttered.

The crowd had already surged closer to the windows. I smelled the woman standing next to me: gin and ice, sweat and dog fever. Torpedo Joe sprinted out of my sight, but I knew he was still ahead. Cathy's chest heaved. She jarred the binoculars against the glass. I put my hand on her hip. The woman next to me started to chant. "Come on, Lacey." Lacey Lady was the favorite. When the dogs turned the final corner, Lacey Lady and Torpedo Joe were neck and neck. I couldn't tell which dog won.

"He won by three noses." She turned, and I dropped my hand.

The announcer boomed out: "A photo finish ..."

"Let's go down to the box while they watch the tape."

We left the booth, walked down the cement steps and passed through the pavilion. They were selling beer, popcorn, hamburgers, Cokes. No lines, just a few people standing around the small tables eating a quick dinner. There was a steady rumble under the pavilion, as if it were filled with people, and the rumble was their voices, but it wasn't full. The floor was littered with losing tickets. It was like walking across a carpet of snow. An old man was bent over by the bathroom doors, picking up the tickets and dropping them in his pockets. He was looking for winners.

While we walked through the pavilion the announcer came on. The winner of the third race ... Cathy froze. She held my arm and laughed. "I love it." She smiled.

Torpedo Joe. Cathy jumped, catching the binoculars before they crashed into her chest. "Another winner. Let's cash in before we go to the box."

I walked to a betting booth, and handed my ticket over. The attendant gathered $347 in his hands. I didn't bother to separate the money.

"How much?" Cathy straightened her dress.

I handed her the money, but she refused. "Three hundred forty-seven," I said and put it in my pocket.

Dr. Fielding sat on a steel table with his left leg propped up and an elbow perched on his knee. He sipped Coke from a plastic cup and watched out the open door as the trainers coaxed their dogs back into the boxes they had come from before the race.

The vet's box was at the end of the track, just behind the starting chutes. The cement wall that kept the fans in their seats sloped off and I could have walked straight onto the track from the box. Dr. Fielding spat ice cubes out the open door. Cathy walked in and hugged him, then sat at the edge of the table. I walked in a second later and shook hands with the doctor.

"Keeping you busy?"

No, he said, then got up and shut the door.

I thought he wanted the money, so I took it out of my pocket, ready to hand it over. Dr. Fielding looked into my face, pretending, I guessed, not to see the wad of cash I was trying to hand him.

"How much, Legget?" He cracked an ice cube in his teeth.

"About two hundred. I bet a little too, so I'll have to split it."

"OK. Why don't you keep it."

"Oh, no. It's your money, I don't mind, here."

"Keep it." He set his cup on the table. "Keep it for later."

Sam knocked on the door, and Cathy got up to let him in. He had Torpedo Joe on a leash. Cathy bent down and jogged the hound's ears, then removed his muzzle. Joe wagged his long, bony tail. Sam nodded to me and smiled at Dr. Fielding. Dr. Fielding took out his stethoscope from a cabinet and listened to Joe's heart.

"Sounds fine." He pulled the scope out of his ears.

Cathy rubbed Joe's back. "Lacey Lady almost had him," she said to Sam.

"They can't beat him. It's all in the training." Sam looked at me.

I thought about the fact that Torpedo Joe had probably been drugged before he raced, and I wondered if that was the kind of training

Sam was talking about. I felt sick. I felt drawn into them. There was a thrill to it all. Being in the back rooms, the underside of the track, knowing which dogs to bet on, knowing who was going to win. They were drawing me in to protect themselves. The money I had won that night was the bribe, and soon they'd toss me out of the circle.

I walked over and rubbed Joe's tense flank. His eyes were brown and soft, like all greyhounds. I could see Cathy loved the dog. She coddled him. He was a racer bred to win. But, I thought, how long does a dog last when it's doped? When he ran as fast as he could on his own legs, then harder with the boil of epinephrine in his blood, pumping his heart like a bellows. How far could a dog like that go?

* * *

Cathy wanted to drive my truck because, she said, it was easier than giving directions. She didn't live far from the track. It was a huge apartment complex on the tip of Clarke Road, near an old gas station with broken windows. When she pulled the truck into a parking space, I started to light a cigar, but she touched my hand with the tip of her fingernail, then ran her finger over the matches, and pushed them away.

"Don't smoke." She looked at me, and the light was odd across her face: a wedge beneath her chin, along her neck and hair.

I put the cigars in the glove compartment, took a deep breath, and noticed how dark it was. There were no lights outside the building or in the corridor where the stairwells and apartment doors were. The building blocked out most of the moon, except for a piece that slipped over the roof. Cathy fiddled with her purse, then sighed. I figured I was supposed to say something. It was that time, but I could think of nothing, so I cleared my throat.

She asked if I wanted to come inside, and I nodded politely. She probably didn't see me nod in the dark, but she must have known, because she slid out of the truck and started up the stairs.

As I walked up the stairs behind her, I felt isolated. A breeze lifted from the ground floor and swirled around. Our shoes scuffled on the cement. We didn't talk. I didn't understand why she wanted me to come up to her apartment. Maybe it was just the way things worked. But we had hardly gotten along. We had different goals. I didn't know her well, but I was sure that sleeping with me wasn't part of any bargain to keep me quiet about Diamond Kennels. That was foolish thinking.

She unlocked the door, and a small white dog burst out, wagging his tail, jumping on her legs. She pulled her skirt away from his claws, then bent and lifted him from the ground. The little dog was so excited I thought he might piss on her, but instead he just licked her face and neck. She half turned, and her eyes softened somehow. Maybe it was the weak light or the dog, but her chin lowered, and the lines on her face didn't seem as hard as they had. I hoped she was relaxing.

"This is Maxwell, but I call him Slick because he can open closed doors and get his food out of the pantry."

I touched Slick's head.

"I'm not surprised you have a dog." I followed her inside the apartment. It smelled like old coffee and incense. There was a blue couch with a blanket folded over the back, next to a short table facing the doorway. A television reflected light from a window at the south end. I walked to the window and parted the curtains. There were dried flowers on the ledge, and below I saw the pool, a soda machine, lawn chairs and tables.

Cathy was in her kitchen scooping kibbles from a bag in the pantry. Slick bounced at her feet, balanced in the air for a second, then fell and bounced again like a white bag of springs.

"I was thinking about taking a dog from the pound," I said while Slick ate his dinner.

"Oh?" She looked up under the hair that obscured her face, then stood, slapping kibble grains from her hands.

"A blue tick hound named Cal. A year old."

"Do you have a yard? That kind of dog needs a lot of room."

"Not yet. I don't have a yard. I live in a trailer. It's like a can of tuna fish, damn shame, respectable man like me living in a trailer." I sat on a chair near the couch.

"Damn respectable man," Cathy said, while moving closer.

"I am in a sense."

"What sense is that?" She sat on the couch and crossed her legs.

"I don't know really." I shrugged.

"Do you want some coffee?" she asked brightly.

She went to the kitchen to make it. We drank coffee in her small living room while listening to music.

We drank more coffee. She made it on the stove with a blue camping percolator. It took longer, but I thought it tasted much better than what I was used to drinking. She looked at her fingers and my lips while we talked. When she looked at my lips, hot flashes went through me. It felt like she was studying me in an approving way, like she was appreciating me. I'm sure she caught me looking at her breasts and her long, tan legs. She left her hands on her thighs, and drummed her fingers against them.

There was the kennel between us. I knew it would be a sensitive area and tried not to open the subject, but it was impossible. The conversation turned when Cathy mentioned the rain we'd been having and then I asked how it affected the greyhounds. She tightened up when I said it. Her legs bunched up a little closer, and her eyes avoided mine.

I finished my cup and walked into the kitchen with Slick on my heels. I rinsed the cup in the sink and put it on the dish rack.

"Look, we don't have to talk about that place right now."

She said bluntly, "I know this is awkward, but I have to understand your position. I'd like to think the kennel's got nothing to do with this evening. But that's stupid." She turned around again. I walked back into the living room and saw her pouting.

"Don't worry," I said. "I should buy you dinner with all this money I won."

"How much was it?" She had her arms over the top of the couch, her chin resting on the back of her hands, feet dangling over the edge.

"Three hundred forty-seven." I pushed Slick away from my leg.

"You could buy me a lot more than dinner."

"Like what?"

"Oh, jewelry, clothes ..."

"Is that really what you want?" I walked closer to her, kneeled in front of the couch.

"No, not really." Her face was close to mine. I felt her breathing.

"Then what?"

"I don't know, to be free somehow."

I kissed her. Her mouth was fresh. Her lips twitched against mine, then I released her.

"I only have three hundred forty-seven dollars." I smiled.

I didn't know if I could have stayed the night or not. But then, I thought the best thing to do was kiss her again while she was letting me. I tasted a touch of alcohol and makeup maybe. Pulling away, I noticed she'd closed her eyes and kept them closed. Posed like she was still kissing. Maybe it had been as long for her as it had for me. She was sitting on the end of the sofa, kind of sideways, with her legs close together. It made the dress pull tight around her thigh, and I leaned back some because my legs were going stiff and I wanted to see as much of her as I could. She had that full shape a woman has that pulls your eye. I couldn't believe I had a chance.

She moved her hand to the sofa and I saw the whole shape of it and its gentle slope and firmness all together. I had to touch it. I just wanted to feel it against the soft parts of my own skin. So I took her hand and kissed the inside of it, then put it against my face and shivered. She had her eyes closed still, but a little smile was there.

"I know that's your face," she said.

"It's so soft," I said, and kissed it again. "And your dress. You look so pretty, I've wanted to tell you all night."

"I haven't worn it in a long time." She opened her eyes and put her other hand against my cheek.

There was nothing better than the way a woman could look at you. It made you forget everything else. You couldn't see anything else and you didn't want to. I got the feeling strong and reached for her bare shoulders, running my hand along her freckles and milky skin. I tried to look in her face and see what she was thinking, if she was going to stop me or if she was OK. But I couldn't tell, and my insides were starting to tremble. Her breathing picked up when my hand followed the curve of her shoulder, then a little lower where I touched the top part of her breast and gripped it some.

That's when I got the feeling the strongest, that first touch and the way her eyes widened when she looked down, like she was surprised just a hand could make her feel something. I wanted to touch as much of her skin as I could and fumbled with the straps of her dress.

She had this crazy look on her face, and I could see her breathing going fast and short. Then she grabbed my shoulders so hard I almost stumbled into the coffee table. She pulled me close and pressed her lips on mine and reached around to the back of my head. Our breathing was mixing and my mind went blank and there was nothing but this sweet rush and flutter.

She pushed me away and I even rolled onto my back and she moved with it and straddled me there on the floor. The dog came over and thought it was his time, but I pushed him away and he went and sat on the chair and watched. Cathy got out of the arm straps and pulled the dress down then reached around to unhook her bra. When it fell loose her breasts tumbled out like pale fruit, beautiful soft mounds with the darkest nipples I'd ever seen. Their movement sent surges of tension and quakes through my spine. My palms and chest ached bad to touch them. But somewhere in the back of my mind I thought this girl had gone wild, that I almost wasn't there. It was the look in her eyes and the frantic way she moved, as if she had to steal as much as she could before it went away.

She leaned forward and offered her sloped breasts to my mouth, grabbed the back of my head again and pulled it closer and leaned down more and buried my face in there. She threw her head back and mumbled something. But I felt trapped beneath her and wanted to get my arms free and have movement and slow down.

But she had a plan and was rubbing herself against my groin and things were getting tight. I almost told her to get up, but I knew if I stopped her everything might stop, and I didn't want that. Maybe this would make a bond, and things would only get better. Because she smelled like oranges and salt and I loved the smell already.

I worked my shirt partway off. When she saw it, she helped me pull it off, then laid herself against my bare chest. I felt her stomach against mine. Her arms were wrapped snug against my sides, and even her legs squeezed against me. I closed my eyes and just let the feeling of her seep in. I was in a warm knot with this soft woman, and nothing had ever felt so good.

I felt her heart against my chest, and the way her pelvis twitched. She started to squeeze her legs harder and rub. I reached down and touched her ass and pushed it against me, then dug through to find my pants. She realized I was squirming out of them and let up some and dug at the zipper. My pants got stuck around my boots, and I was kicking at them until she mounted me again. She'd taken her panties off too, and I felt her wet mound and scratchy pubic hair and the hard bone of her pelvis.

She reached back and aimed me inside, and I slid in and lurched up, grabbing her shoulders through all of her hair that fell down and hung between us. I clenched her shoulders and pulled her down, then wrapped my arms around her back and hugged her close, kind of pumping her with my arms in a bear hug. She started moaning, and it sounded far off because my own head was just explosions and color. All my blood was going to one place. I don't know how long we stayed like that, but my arms were slick with sweat, and it felt hot in the room, and I was so tired, I could barely open my eyes until she pulled up and smoothed her dress and grabbed the little dog.

I felt a draft when she walked away, and I opened my eyes. She was in the kitchen with the little dog in her arms and her dress already back on straight.

"Hey," I said. "What's wrong?"

"No, nothing," she said. But I saw she was lying.

I leaned up and found my pants at my ankles to pull them on and wondered what had gone wrong. Maybe things had happened too fast for her. It could be like that for women. I got the pants up and buttoned, and walked over to where she stood. She was cleaning the percolator while Slick sat on the counter and watched. I moved up behind her and put my arms around her waist, kissed her shoulder. I felt her tense up.

"Look, I'm sorry if I did the wrong thing."

"No, you didn't. I wanted to."

"Yeah, then what's wrong?"

"It's just how I feel sometimes, like I should know better, have more control. You understand?"

I backed up and leaned against the other counter, stretched my back some and wondered.

"I think so, Cathy. I want to see you again."

She turned, and Slick yapped a little.

"OK, of course. I want that too," she said.

I didn't know how real it was, but I wasn't going to analyze it. I felt good and spent. Whatever happened, I was there and knew I had a chance. I also knew it was better sometimes not to say a thing.

Chapter 5

I wished the body truck had a CB so I could call Molly Phelps and find out if the inspector had arrived. John had said on the phone that today was the day, but he hadn't told me who or when. There were no strange cars in the parking lot, so I drove back to the incinerator and parked the truck. I walked back to the kennel and let Cal out of his cage. The kennel had just been cleaned, and the floors were wet and shiny. Cal's paws were wet, and his tail sprayed water when he shook it. He bolted out the back door, and I tried to yell him to a stop, but he was too excited. For a second, I thought he was gone, that he had run off because I had abandoned him for too long. When I stepped outside, though, he was waiting for me.

I jogged with him a ways through the grass, and felt a breeze that carried with it some of the smell from the incinerator. Orange and white wildflowers had grown at the edge of the fence. They were just weeds, but they reminded me of Ragtime Kennel, and seeing those same flowers at the edge of the building, just as bright and clear as these. Cal wanted to run, to stretch his cramped legs and enjoy the outside. And I couldn't help but think of two years ago, the greyhounds.

The kennel was called Ragtime. It was out on Airport Road, which was a lonely stretch filled with abandoned warehouses and storage facilities. Below a billboard was a short, white building with old-time casement windows.

I couldn't tell if there was a front door behind the weeds. I parked my truck where I thought there might be an entrance and lit my last cigar, turned off the engine and listened. Nothing to hear but the wind blowing through the weeds and shrubs, bunting itself against the peeled paint and cracked boards. It was a good spot for vagrants. I was more than a little worried that I had found the wrong place. But I hadn't.

It was the kind of place you noticed on your way to work while you waited at a stop light. It made you think about how things faded. You could see the building crumble, disappearing, and you wanted to go and see it once, before it fell. You wanted to get a taste of what it had been. Since it was near the airport you might have thought it was an aviation warehouse and maybe you'd find an old tool or a propeller blade. You'd take it home, clean it, and hang it on the wall. That was the kind of place it was.

I got out of the truck. My boots sunk into the deep grass. I walked around the side to a window and looked through it. The window was huge, three times the size of a window in a house, and it was busted out at the bottom; the glass at the top just kind of hung there, and I imagined it falling on my neck. So I just peeked in at the bottom. A breeze picked up and blew. My shirt billowed and my hair lifted back a little ways. It was dark inside, too dark to see anything, it was the kind of dark that multiplies with walls and doorways, the kind you can't see through. When the breeze rushed out of the building, it was thicker and smelled sweet. I had smelled it before, and it sickened me.

I ducked down from the window, the quickest way out of that breeze, and fell on my knees in the grass. I had the dry heaves, and a whole set of memories from Animal Control came back, then I wiped them away because I couldn't think of those things. But I did remember how John had told me about doing what was right, doing what had to be done, because no one else would. I was the person who had to walk in there first, and see what had to be seen. So I walked around the edge of the building looking for a doorway. Around the side, the space opened and there was a field that stretched to the airport runway. I saw the lights and the radar tower in the distance.

The grass and weeds had been trampled, and I could tell someone had tried at one point to mow it down, but the mower's path stopped, leaving a stripe in the middle of the tall grass. A path was worn by the door, and the dirt had been kicked up under a cement slab in front of it. A sign had been there, but now it was a square of color impossible to read.

I pushed open the door with my boot, and it was still too dark to see. I thought of yelling for an answer but decided not to. My throat was dry and had tightened up, and I probably couldn't have yelled if I'd had to. I stood still for a moment and let my eyes adjust to the light.

The building separated into two main hallways that ran toward the back. I put my hand in front of my face, took a step forward and felt a damp wall. I pulled my hand away quickly, and wiped it on my pants. I took small breaths so the smell wasn't as bad.

There was something inside. It had a pulse. It was like when you went into a house and somehow you could sense there was someone inside it. You felt the breathing on your skin. You counted the heartbeats you thought you heard.

I stepped forward. My eyes had adjusted well, and my boots felt solid on the hard floor. But the heat came up through the leather, and they filled with sweat. The air was stifling. The first room looked like a horse stall. The walls were made of two-by-fours, the skeleton of a full wall with cut wires and empty sockets. I stepped in something damp and almost slipped. I reached for the wall which was near my waist and grabbed it. I felt a nylon rope beneath my fingers. It was taut, so I pulled it.

A weak, dry growl rolled from the darkness. At first, I wasn't sure, but the sound was close. It all connected just then; it was the only sound in the world.

It was too dark to go further, but I was compelled to touch the dog, to force myself to believe it was real, to know that someone could leave a hound in that foul darkness.

I took my lighter from my pants pocket and fumbled with the flint. The yellow light opened a circle of floating dust. I saw a fuse box on the wall, a few steps away, so I switched on the lights. Carnival lights: four, five, six bulbs popped on in rows down the hallway.

The greyhounds shuffled, some tried to stand, others lay on the floor, unmoving. They wore muzzles and had moist, round eyes. The greyhound at the end of the rope stood between three younger hounds. The large greyhound was toothless and panting. Her head sagged down near an empty steel bowl covered with red ants. Her teats hung from her thin belly. I let go of the rope and stepped around the rotten stall door. The floor was covered with excrement.

They had kept her tied in there to nurse the pups. They may

have been her own, but she was emaciated, and I didn't think she was capable of doing it. Her ribs stuck out so far they looked like tent poles. I unwrapped the rope from her neck. There was a fleshy groove where it had been. She looked up, ears pinned back, and then her tail moved slightly from side to side. Fleas crawled across her skin. I brushed them away, but they just scurried to her belly.

The lights were draped over cross-beams above the hallway. I saw five stalls, each like the first. In the second stall two hounds lay on the cement. One was black, the other a muddy silver. I thought they both were dead. Their eyes didn't open when I coughed and their chests were still. My eyes watered and stung.

After the four stalls, at the end of the hallway near a large, aluminum door, there were three stacks of plastic airline cages. Most of them were orange, covered with dirt or blood or feces. The dogs in these cages pressed their snouts against the wire doors. They didn't have enough room to stand or turn around. It made my knees and chest ache with such an empty, dull pain. I felt their claustrophobia. I opened the cage doors, hoping they would crawl out, then walked back to the stalls. I found another bitch tied to a pile of cement blocks. She wagged her tail and licked my hand when I touched her. Kneeling closer, I felt her teats. They were hard as rocks. Her milk had dried up.

I left the building, and radioed Molly Phelps. She dispatched the other officers. My voice was weak and sullen, not my own. She said John was on his way.

We had piled twenty-six dead greyhounds outside the front door. Some of the bodies were weeks old. Seventeen volunteers from the Humane

Society helped clean the kennel. They were young, mostly teenagers, and they had never seen anything like that before. When they first piled out the back of the blue pickup truck, they were loud and anxious. After they saw the inside of the kennel, they worked in silence, their heads down. They had trouble getting used to the masks.

The dog catchers filled their trucks and transported the live greyhounds to three different veterinarians. There were ten still living. Most were put to sleep. They had suffered in the darkness and heat long past the chance of recovery. Only the very strongest survived the hookworm, starvation, heat, and neglect.

When the kennel had been cleaned out, the photographs taken, my statements recorded, and the search for clues as to the identity of the owner finished, I rode with John to the nearest bar to fill my stomach.

That was where we found the owner. He must have noticed our uniforms as we entered the bar, then heard us talking. It was a small place with two canoe paddles on a brown wall, five tables, and a long bar with wobbly stools. It smelled like urine, human urine, different than an animal's.

We had to harden ourself against the feeling. That was the only way. And it was a private kind of swallowing we did. Only another person who had seen what we had seen could understand it. You needed the smell on your fingers, the taste of sweat and fur in your mouth, the blood and shit on your boots. That was the only way.

The kennel owner must have wanted to free himself. Something I would never understand was why he hadn't asked for help before his world fell apart. Whatever his reasons, he stood up from the end of the bar and shuffled across the dirty floor, his eyes wild, his shirt hanging off his shoulders. When he got close to our table, before I had even seen him coming, I smelled him. I had thought it was another dog catcher or a volunteer, but John's face told me different. The man's hair was black and matted against his sunburned forehead. His shoulders and arms were covered with tiny, white boils. He set his beer on the table between us, gently pulled his shirt around his shoulders, becoming dignified. He introduced himself as the owner of the kennel.

John grabbed him by the shoulders and tugged him outside. The bartender jumped, ready to stop something, but I stood and walked to the bar, pulling money from my pockets for our unfinished drinks. When I got outside, John's anger had turned to arms and fists. The greyhounder was slumped, belly down, over the hood of John's truck. His head clunked off the hood from John's punches. The bartender followed me outside and stood with a look in his eyes that said, I've seen this before, but now you have to stop.

"John," I said quietly. In the bar, the dogman had been a servant of evil. Now, I realized he was nothing more than a weak man.

"John, that's enough." I stood behind him.

John had torn the man's shirt. He let go of the greyhounder, who fell to the dirt. He muttered to himself, to us maybe. When I saw the trainer's head cocked against the front tire, my anger seeped away. What I saw in his face was bliss. I knew then, he had wanted punishment.

* * *

I stroked Cal's head, and remembered how much I had wanted to keep that greyhound in the first stall. She had survived mastitis and gastrointestinal rot. That dog had been strong. I had wanted to make up for the cruelty she had endured. I would never forget how she had wagged her tail when I untied her. She'd walked out of that hell-pit on needle-thin legs, but she walked, leaning into my leg.

I imagined Cal living in my trailer. I pictured him in the square bedroom with the sloping ceiling, the miniature kitchen, and the shoebox living room. I wondered what he would do all day while I was working, and decided I couldn't leave him in the trailer. It was too hot in the afternoon, and Cal was the kind of dog that needed to be outside. I was the kind of man who needed a dog that needed to be outside.

I stretched out on the grass to play with him, but jumped up quickly, remembering the inspector. I thought I should look decent. I went inside to check the time, and ran into John on his way out.

"Good timing. He's here." John held the door open.

I looked at his face, and it seemed calm, almost uninterested.

"Who is it?"

He rubbed his neck. He couldn't help but break into a cat-and-mouse smile. "You won't believe me, but it's Dario and his partner."

Dario. I liked it. He had been there when it happened. But if Dario was the investigator, that meant there might be a criminal charge. If there wasn't that possibility, the inspector would have been some clerk from the Palm County government.

I followed John to his office. Dario stood in the doorway in civilian clothes. He had his hair slicked back and wore a red tie and silver cuff links. He turned around. His tie clip was a pair of tiny handcuffs. It made me nervous. The look on his face made me nervous. He wasn't the joking, sweaty sheriff I had come to know. Dario looked serious and official.

"What happened to your clothes?" I asked.

"Got promoted. You remember my partner."

It was the blonde lady with the perfect uniform. She carried a legal pad and a tape recorder. She didn't seem quite as serious as Dario. In fact, she shook my hand, and smiled. No, she looked all right.

"Well, let's get started." Dario shrugged.

John took them into his office while I waited outside. He closed the door, walked over to me, and put his hands on my shoulders. His breath smelled like tobacco.

"Legget, listen to me." His eyes narrowed; he took a deep breath. "I'm on your side. I always have been."

"I thought this was just routine?"

"I thought so too. I don't understand what's going on. But I got to tell you, it feels strange."

"Great." I walked into John's office with his voice in my head.

Dario was sitting on the couch and his partner, Elaine, was behind the desk fiddling with the tape recorder. She blew into the microphone. "I never say testing 1,2,3." She placed it on the desk, then aimed it at me.

I sat on an aluminum chair facing the desk. Dario was on my left. I didn't look at him.

Elaine turned on the recorder, asked my name and address. She told the recorder who she was and where we were, the date, the time.

"So this is what happens when you do what you're told," I said.

"Wrong place, wrong time." Dario shifted, pulled his coattails from underneath him.

"Is it criminal? Hey, turn it off for a second." I reached over the desk.

Elaine looked at Dario and he waved his hand. She turned it off.

"Listen, Dario. What's going on?"

"What do you mean?"

"Stop playing cop and tell me what's up."

"It's hard to explain." He scratched his chin.

"Try!"

"It's all a big fuck-up."

Elaine opened her purse, found a cigarette, and lit it. She leaned back and blew smoke rings. "Strange things happen in city government," she said.

Dario continued. "You remember Ms. Holton of course. We responded to a call. I told you. A break-in. I got there late; I was there for the curtain only."

"So was I."

"Well, that was a surprise. You see, I thought at the most, I'd call you on a signal 7. You'd come get the body and be out of there. But the dog wasn't dead."

"Wait a minute," I interrupted. Something was wrong. How would he know the dog was going to be dead? "I don't understand, Dario. Signal 7 is for a body pickup, not a vicious animal."

"Legget, we've gone into this far enough. Man, look, all I know, and all I care to know, is that the dog was supposed to be dead, and I was supposed to call Animal Control. I just picked you because I was told you were OK. I'm sorry I did now, but how could I predict this?"

"The dog's not rabid Dario."

"So?"

"So there would be no need to kill it. Is that standard procedure?"

"Hell, no" He sat up. "Turn the recorder on," he snapped to Elaine.

"Legget, I'm going to tell you one thing, and then it's over. Do you understand?" He held his hand in the air for Elaine to wait. My head was spinning. I didn't understand this at all. "Certain people wanted Ms. Holton to be punished. I don't know why, and I don't care. But it's all about that. Legget, it's just the way the world is. You're supposed to be cool." Then he gave me a look with his eyebrows raised and smirked like I shouldn't worry too much.

Elaine turned the recorder on, and I thought about how the world was.

Chapter 6

Calling Cathy's apartment on John's phone, I got her answering machine. I stayed on the line just to listen to her voice. Maybe I needed someone to cry to about my problems at Animal Control. Maybe I didn't want to lose too many things at one time. But whatever the reasons were right then, I got Cal out of his cage with the intention of going to her.

John sat in the reception room waiting with his legs crossed and picked at his pipe. He had a thoughtful, concerned look on his face, and I sat down next to him. I let Cal go off and explore.

"Seems as if I've got caught up in somebody else's bullshit."

"We're both getting caught up in it." He put his pipe on a small magazine stand.

"Dario told me some things. They're making paper on it."

"Paperwork. Goddamn job's full of it. What else?"

"He said it was supposed to be a signal 7."

"What do you mean?" He looked up.

"I don't know exactly, but Dario said that the dog was supposed to be dead when he got there, and his job was to call me. He said something about revenge. Some kind of punishment that someone wanted to inflict on the woman."

"Jesus. The dog was supposed to be dead?"

"That's what he said."

"You know what that means? It doesn't sound right, but it means one thing."

"Somebody was supposed to kill her dog."

"That is some malicious shit." He picked up his pipe, then stood. The chair shook against my leg. I watched him pace the floor, rubbing his head, switching his pipe from his hand to his pocket. "I got to think about this. This means something."

"It means I'm probably out of a job because somebody didn't like Ms. Holton."

"I won't let them do it." John stopped pacing and looked me in the eye. It felt like a challenge, like he was testing my ability to fight.

"What can we do about it?" I stood up too. I heard the dogs barking in the kennel behind us. Tom and Albert must have started the afternoon feeding. Cal poked his head around the corner of the open door.

"Hey, Cal," Cal wagged his tail, and tried to sniff out John's pipe. "I'm not sure what we can do right now, Legget."

"Maybe I could talk to Dario, away from here." I squatted, and Cal bounded over.

"How about Gant?" John sat down, then leaned forward on his legs.

"What's Gant got to do with this?"

"I don't know." He started to light his pipe.

"If you want me to talk to him ..."

"No, I just thought out loud." He blew smoke into the air. Cal flinched. "Listen, if you want to work today it's fine. I never should have stopped you in the first place."

"How about tomorrow?" Cal tried to pull away, so I held his collar.

* * *

When I pulled onto the kennel road, I saw four trucks parked in front of the buildings and regretted coming there. It looked as if they were having a meeting of some sort, and that was strange because I had never heard of different kennels getting together for anything other than a race.

I knew how ridiculous it would be for me to drive up in an Animal Control truck and start walking around, but I figured I would find Cathy, then take her for coffee or something. I parked under an oak tree that shaded the gravel path, hoping to obscure my bright orange truck, and wrapped a blue leash around Cal's neck. The three greyhound trucks were filled with dogs. I smelled them in the hot cages. I wondered how those dogs lived through it. Cal pulled away, and tried to worm out from under the leash, but I held it tightly and was firm with him.

I walked up to the cages. The hackles on Cal's back rose slightly when the greyhounds jumped to the sides of their cages. Cathy came out of the back shed pushing a wheelbarrow stacked high with stainless steel bowls filled with meat and covered with a peppering of flies.

She noticed me, and dropped the legs of the wheelbarrow, then ran over with an awkward, pretty smile on her face.

"What are you doing here, Legget?" She sounded anxious.

"Came to see you, and show you Cal."

"Oh, Jesus. This is a bad time."

"Why?"

"Just help me get these bowls out. Tie him up, hurry."

I walked Cal closer to the cages and tied his leash to a metal pole. I knelt down near his face, and he looked nervous. His brow was wrinkled over his eyes, and he started to pant. I rubbed his cheeks, and his head and told him I'd be right back. I followed Cathy to the wheelbarrow, and saw it was horse meat. It was piled in bloody lumps in the bowls. It smelled rotten, and I saw white veins the size of snakes, twisted in the flesh.

"God, this is awful."

"It's got peaches in it! Come on."

I pushed the wheelbarrow while Cathy pulled off the bowls and gave them to the dogs.

"It thawed out a little more than it's supposed to," she said while we turned the corner, and I lost sight of Cal.

"What's going on here?"

"It's just a meeting. We'll finish before they get out."

"Is Sam in there?"

"Of course, let's hurry, please." She swatted at the flies hovering around us.

There were only four bowls left when I heard a door slam, and then two, maybe three voices yelling, "Go around, grab him, hurry." Cathy dropped the bowl she had in her hand, looked at me, then ran around the side of the building, where the aloe plants grew.

I left the wheelbarrow and followed her. When I turned the corner I saw Sam standing on top of Cal. Cal was lying on his side in the grass, breathing too hard. I darted toward him. Sam looked up when Cathy yelled to him, and he must've seen me charging him because he backed away from Cal, a confused look on his face. I dove into him, throwing all my weight into my right shoulder, and I knew I hit him square because I heard all the breath shoot out of his mouth, and then he groaned painfully. I landed on him when he hit the ground. I rolled and jumped to my feet.

"What did you do to him?" The other greyhounders were on the other side of the building, about thirty feet away, running toward me.

Sam didn't answer. I looked at Cal, and he was still down. I kicked Sam once in the face with the flat end of my boot. His nose burst with blood like a little balloon. I turned around and went to Cal.

One of the greyhounders reached me while I bent over to lift Cal off the ground. He had chewed through his leash, and part of it was hanging from his neck. He started whimpering, and I talked to him, but the greyhounder grabbed my shoulders and spun me around and punched me twice in the face. I couldn't see well, so I just threw myself forward, into the shape of him, and started pulling and punching. I was much stronger: a few punches and he was backing away, and I hadn't even risen from my knees.

I heard Cathy behind me, but I was afraid to turn my back on the greyhounder. He was a short, bald man with a big gut and a knife case on his cut-off jeans. I was worried about the knife case.

Someone touched my back, and I whirled, ready to fight, but it was

Cathy, and her face was pinched up, her eyes red as blood, and she had her hands over her ears.

"We've got to take him."

I lifted Cal, and when I did, he yelped with the pain. I cried when I had to walk past the greyhounders and Sam who was mopping the blood from his face with someone's white shirt. Cathy held my arm and supported Cal's head while we walked to my truck.

"Fuck you Sam!" she screamed.

"I thought it was wild, Cathy. I was protecting our dogs!" he yelled back, but we kept walking because Cal was hurt bad. I put Cal in one of my cages and told Cathy to get inside the truck. I gave her the keys, and walked back to Sam.

"No, Legget." Cathy said from inside the truck.

The greyhounders had formed a half circle around Sam. I walked toward them.

"Tell me what you did."

"I found him running around my cages. I thought he was wild. I didn't know he was yours."

"What did you do!"

"Kicked him, in the chest, you fucking bastard."

I ran back to my truck, got inside, then whipped it around. Cathy had already started the engine.

"Why did you come here ..." She muttered, but I didn't answer. I drove to Dr. Fielding, trying to avoid the bumps and turns so Cal didn't bounce around in the cage.

I carried Cal through the back entrance of Dr. Fielding's hospital and put him on top of a metal tub. I could feel a spot against his ribs where his breath sucked in at his skin and bone. Dr. Fielding charged out of his office with Cathy close behind. He looked at Cal's gums, felt his chest, then ran his fingers over his spine.

"Hit by a car?" He asked.

"Kicked."

Dr. Fielding leaned against the sink just behind him, pushed his glasses up his nose, and clicked his tongue. He was completely calm. Cathy stood next to him wringing her hands together. A sweat had broken on her forehead.

"Susan!" Dr. Fielding leaned to the side and yelled up a hallway at the front of his hospital. He crossed his arms, and looked at Cal. Susan emerged from the hallway, a heavy woman wearing a flowered smock.

"Sorry, Dr. Fielding." She set her magazine down. "I didn't hear them come in."

I knew Susan from the times I had been there before. She was supposed to be a good technician.

"That's OK. Get that oxygen tent ready."

Susan walked toward the cages at the back of the hospital.

"Flail chest." He said while picking an amber bottle filled with medicine from the shelf behind him. "Shock first, oxygen, a little of this Azium, then we'll see. Hold his leg." He said to Cathy.

The doctor found a vein in Cal's front leg, and inserted the needle. He drew back a pinch of blood, then plunged the clear, syrup-like fluid into his vein.

"Is this is an Animal Control case?"

"No, doc. This is my dog. Go all the way."

"OK. Don't get excited. Why don't you go clean yourself up." He pointed toward the bathroom. I knew where it was.

I had purple knuckle-prints across my cheeks and under my eyes where the greyhounder's fist had connected. I was sure I was going to have at least one black eye. I ran the water and splashed it over my face. It was cold. It opened my eyes. I looked into the mirror.

I couldn't explain the feeling just then, but it was a feeling of being alone, like I was the only person in the world that would do anything to save that dog. But, I couldn't do a thing. I tried to imagine what John would tell me. I closed my eyes and pictured his face. The puffed cheeks, the slightly slanted eyes. His brown skin and black beard with a stripe of grey under the chin. He might have told me there was a hole inside my chest big enough to drive a truck through. What are you going to do to fill it up?

They had removed Cal from the tub and put him in the oxygen tent. Cathy sat on the floor in front of the clear plastic cover where a tube ran through a hole, and pumped fresh oxygen into the cage where Cal lay. They had connected a bag of fluids, and it ran, wide open, into Cal's leg.

I stood above Cathy and looked through the tent. His eyes were closed. He took deep, heavy breaths, as if he couldn't get enough air. If he was a dog I had just picked up on the street, Dr. Fielding would have put him down. Animal Control couldn't pay for fluids, oxygen, and the X-rays I knew were sure to follow.

I led Cathy away from the cage, then hugged her. She felt warm, and moved into my arms. I held her shoulders, and looked at her for a moment. I studied her rich brown eyes, the swollen cheeks that formed deep lines around her eyes and mouth. Her hair fell around her shoulders and touched my fingers. Her lip trembled slightly.

"We're going to have to talk when I get back."

She nodded and averted her eyes. She knew what I meant.

"Can you stay here a while until the X-rays come out?"

"Yes, I can stay."

I let go of her shoulders and leaned against the freezer. It was the same freezer I had emptied so many times. It was warm, and it vibrated against my back.

"I'm sorry this happened, Legget."

I touched the side of her head and squeezed a clump of her soft hair. "I am too, but it's not your fault. You know that. In fact, it's mine."

I don't think she completely understood what I meant, but it didn't matter.

I drove Cathy home when Dr. Fielding wanted to close the hospital and Cal was off the oxygen. Dr. Fielding made arrangements with Susan to come to the clinic twice during the night and check on Cal. They had taken the oxygen tent away, and he had been breathing normally for two hours. Dr. Fielding assured me that Cal would be fine, and I'd probably take him home the next day. I wasn't sure where I was going to take him.

I sat in the truck with Cathy in front of her apartment building. There were black circles under her eyes, and her cheeks kind of sagged from her ears down. I tried to apologize, but I didn't quite know what to apologize for. Maybe, for going to the kennel in the first place. But Cathy didn't think I had done anything wrong. She seemed distant and dreamy. Something else was on her mind.

"Is it your brother?"

"Sam," she said. "Sam isn't a problem. Look, do you want to come up?"

"No, I think I need to go home tonight. Can I call you? I'm sorry about all this, Cathy. You've been a big help."

She nodded and took my hand, then kissed me on the cheek. She pressed an envelope into my front pocket, and I flinched away.

"What's this?"

"Take it home, then call me if you want to."

"OK." I watched her walk up the stairs to her apartment.

* * *

I felt like it was the first time in months that I had spent the evening in my trailer alone. For a second, as I cruised up the narrow street, I forgot where I lived. The porch lights weren't on, and I tried to remember if I had switched them on when I had left. Moonlight reflected off the silver flank of the trailer, and I thought that was a good welcoming.

It was hot inside. I ducked under the bookshelf and turned on the air conditioning. The ceiling in my trailer was a little lower than a ceiling in an apartment or a house. When you got near the ends, north or south, it sloped down and curved into a wall. At these spots, if you weren't short, you had to duck down. The air conditioner was nestled in the wall beneath a one-shelf bookcase that went from wall to wall. I had a small collection of used books and magazines. Mostly, I had picked up magazines here and there, at convenience stores when I was working and went inside for a pack of Sweets or a soda.

I opened the refrigerator and grabbed a cold fifth of Dewars. I liked it cold. It made the first glass go down a little easier, and it was a perfect night for drinking. I flicked on the small radio on the kitchen counter, and I tuned it to the country station, turned it real low.

I found a 7-Eleven cup on the counter, rinsed it in the sink and filled it with ice cubes. I had good water in the trailer. It wasn't that well water that smelled like rotten eggs, but city water which had no taste at all. I filled the plastic cup to the top, and the ice cubes cracked. I set the cup on the coffee table next to the couch. It was a green contraption with a bed inside. It had come with the trailer, and I had never opened it to see how the bed was, though I had fallen asleep on it many times.

I sat on the couch and pulled off my boots and socks, rubbing my feet on the carpet. The television looked dead and grey, but I decided not to turn it on because I hardly ever watched it, and when I did turn it on, it fascinated me, and I got so absorbed in it, I forgot about everything else.

Like Cathy, for one. What was I going to do about her? I had promised we would have a talk, but she had disappeared. And then I remembered the note she had left for me. I had left it in the goddamn truck. Too many things on my mind. I went outside to find it; it had fallen on the floorboards. It had a boot print across it. I brought it inside and sat back down on the couch. It was getting nice and cool inside.

I took a sip of whiskey, and it didn't have much taste, so I took a long swallow and it went straight to my stomach like a fist. The first drink was like that. Then later, every sip would taste like sugar. That was the good part. The sleepy feelings just came on with a taste of sugar in your mouth.

I opened the letter. It had Dr. Fielding's name and address at the top, a script Rx, and then the hospital's name: Dexter's Field Animal Hospital. Dexter's Field was the name given to the land where the hospital was located. It was the site of a Civil War disaster involving Colonel Dexter, but I had never heard of such a man, other than from Dr. Fielding.

Cathy's handwriting was neat and crisp. She had printed my name at the top of the page, then: *I know you suspect me of being involved with something you may not completely approve of. And I want to say there's more to it than that. Some things you cannot change. Cath.*

I read the note twice. It didn't make much more sense the second time than it did the first. But clearly she was trying to tell me something. She wanted to confess. When I thought of confession, I thought of the trainer from Ragtime Kennel, and how the beating John Leland had given him somehow helped him live with what he had done to the dogs. Maybe Cathy wanted the same thing. I didn't think of beating her. But maybe she wanted to rid herself of whatever guilt was attached to her life then. I wasn't sure I was the right one to save her, to listen to the confession, and pronounce a cure. I didn't have any cures. But I liked her. She was a strong girl, and strong girls had a way of taking care of themselves. I went to call her.

My phone was in the bedroom. It was a cheap, plastic phone that sounded like a sick cat when it rang. I hadn't wanted a phone, but John had insisted I get one. I took a cigar to the bedroom and left my drink on the coffee table.

It rang twice before she answered.

"Hey, Cath."

"Hello."

"Well, I'm all settled in. How's Slick?"

"Fine. He chewed up a pair of my shoes today."

"He must have been hungry."

"Did you read my note?"

"Sure, I read it."

"What?"

"I read it, and to tell you the truth I don't completely understand."

"I know it's strange."

"You just open your mouth ..."

"Fuck you, cowboy." She laughed, then cleared her throat.

"Maybe you could help me out, maybe I'll buy you a new pair of shoes. They weren't expensive were they?"

"They were sandals, that's all. Slick's worth a few of those. I don't wear them much anyway."

"No I guess not."

"Legget, did you think Diamond Kennel was a clean place?"

"I thought it was clean. The dogs looked healthy."

"Well it is, and you're right to say that. But, you didn't see all of Diamond Kennel."

"What did I miss?" I thought about the crate of testosterone and wondered if that was what she was referring to.

"The farm."

Chapter 7

I called Susan that night at Dr. Fielding's hospital. Fielding had arranged for her to be there at 10:30 and 2 a.m. She answered the phone like she was supposed to and reported that Cal was breathing fine and seemed hungry. She said we would have to wait till tomorrow before giving him any food.

I had finished the cup of Dewars, stripped, and stretched out on my bed. Cathy had told me on the phone that Diamond Kennel supported not only the dogs I had seen a few days ago but a breeding farm in the woods behind the kennel. She had told me the best dogs made it up the hill. All the racers lived at the main kennel. The ones that didn't win were shipped back to the farm or put to sleep. If they could stud well, and they were needed, they might get back to the farm. I had asked her if I could see it, but she was definitely against the idea. She didn't see how I could without Sam finding out. He was protective of the property.

I was surprised, but not so much that I didn't believe it. Fact was that Cathy felt the need to tell me it was there, and that meant it probably would not have passed my inspection. My head was clouded with drink and the fact that I had to make a decision. I wouldn't have my job at Animal Control too much longer unless John came up with something. And the chances of that happening were slim. Without my uniform, and the county to back me up, what was I? A concerned citizen? A watchdog for the community?

I let myself drift into sleep and knew tomorrow was going to be one hell of a day. One hell of a wild day, and somewhere inside me, I smiled. I liked the idea. I liked the challenge.

* * *

First thing in the morning I called John. Beth answered the phone, and I spoke to her for a few minutes. She asked what had happened to John, and I tried to explain everything the best I could. She said it was strange that he hadn't talked about it, because he always told her about work whether she wanted to hear it or not.

"I suspect I'll being seeing you soon, Beth."

"I'm making pies today." There was an awkward pause, and we hung up.

I showered and dressed in my uniform, called Dr. Fielding's hospital while I tugged on a shirt, but the line was busy. It was a little before 8:00 a.m. I loaded myself into the truck and drove to the 7-Eleven on the corner. They had just started selling that boutique coffee, hazelnut and vanilla creme with fancy cups of flavored half and half. I liked mine black. It was the only way to clear out the throat and kick start the day.

It was a cool morning. The roads were damp from rain, and the traffic was light. I flicked on the CB, but something was wrong. I just got a load of static with tracers, so I shut it off. There was a pack of

Sweets on the bench, wedged between the cushion. I pulled one out and rolled down the window. As it cranked down, I noticed that my truck smelled like Cathy. That orange scent had lingered. I wondered if I should have called her, but it was too early. I planned on seeing her sometime soon. I wasn't sure how, or in what capacity, friend or foe, but I was sure it would happen.

I passed by Greenhorns and saw John's truck parked in the front. Greenhorns was popular in the mornings. I parked, grabbed my phone, and went inside. The place smelled like maple syrup and aftershave. John sat in his booth, staring out a large window at the side of the table. He rubbed his fingers through his beard. The place was crowded. Most of the noise came from the kitchen and the waitresses as they clanked dishes and dunked ice cubes and called up their orders.

"Morning, John." I slid into the booth.

"Legget. It's good to see you this morning. I was just thinking …"

"Let me guess."

"Of course. Want some coffee?"

"Sure."

Dee brought over another cup, and I helped myself. The pot was half empty.

"You been here long?" I blew steam off the cup.

"A while."

"I talked to Beth this morning."

"She's making pies today." He tapped his cup with a finger.

"That's what she said."

John poured himself another cup, filled it with cream and three packs of sugar. He stirred a lot longer than he usually did.

"What's on your mind?" I asked.

"OK. I've just been thinking about you."

"Don't waste too much of your time. What have you been thinking about?" I sipped my coffee.

"I talked to Dr. Fielding this morning."

"Why'd you do that?"

John sat up, stretched his shoulders. "I had two reasons. One, I wanted to see how your dog was doing, and two, I wanted some advice on what to do about our problem."

"How's Cal?"

"Fine. He wants you to pick him up today. Take him home, whatever."

"I didn't think he would make it at first, but he's a tough dog. Young and hardy." I checked my phone to make sure it wasn't blinking.

"Legget, I was prepared, even crazy with the idea of saving your job. It kept me up late last night. I wasn't going to let them do this to you. You're my friend, have been for a long time, and I thought I knew you, but I don't."

"What's changed?"

"I bet you could guess." He shook his head in disapointment.

"Maybe you should tell me straight up."

"OK, Fielding told me about the body tour. Jesus, man, you've corrupted half of Palm County with this shit. I'm not even mad anymore. I'm just shocked, disappointed."

What do you say when you're caught? It was a funny thing. It had taken me a long time to decide if I was crazy or just stupid for what I had been doing with the body tour. For a long time, I had convinced myself that I had a good reason. That I was saving the money for a home, and as soon as I got enough I'd quit and do things right.

But I knew it wasn't about that. Maybe, I'd known it all along. And for some reason I couldn't stop. It had been too easy, and profitable. But was it just the money? For a time, I had believed it was my chance to get part of the action. The veterinarians were making money off of death and disease. Maybe, I should have prayed for the dead animals instead of selling them, but I figured somebody had already done that. Some family, or some child, had cried for the death of its pet. And I was just taking part in the ritual. Money and death.

My phone blinked. I looked at John. He looked at his coffee cup. There was a sadness in his face that I didn't want to look at. Hell, I didn't much care about getting caught, maybe I had wanted to, just like Cathy, like Ragtime Kennel, like everybody else in the whole fucking world. But I had hurt John. That was the part that dug inside my chest and clawed a piece of it away.

"I guess it's over." I set the phone down and pushed the coffee away.

John stared at the table. His cheek trembled. I didn't know if it was anger. "I've thought about it all morning. It kind of turned everything upside down when I talked to Fielding. He's a good old boy, Legget. Here I was trying to figure out how to save your job, and then this. It seems like an easy way out, just to terminate you and all the problems are solved. The Holton case goes away. The body tour goes away, and Legget, you're just gone."

Chapter 8

My trailer seemed empty and dry and hot even with the air conditioning on. I tried reading a magazine, an old *Life* with photographs of Nixon and the police, but it wasn't as interesting as it had seemed when I had first found it in a cardboard box at the curb ready for the trash collectors.

I decided to take a walk, think things through. So I put on a pair of red shorts with bleach stains and a spot of yellow paint; I couldn't remember how it got there. It had been a while since I had worn shorts, and my legs were pale.

I walked deeper into the trailer park, down a one-lane tar road with no gutters. Trailers were packed in on both sides, cars in the road, broken bicycles, cats digging through the trash cans, dogs tied to front steps. The dogs crawled under the skirts of the trailers to stay out of the heat. A brown retriever growled at me from under a rusty double-wide with black iron bars on its windows.

The road cut through the back of the trailer park. There were about fifty trailers in all, twelve down my street. Mine was the last one on the left, closest to the road. I passed the trash dumpster, about as far as I had ever gone on foot. I noticed a couple of brown kids playing by a chicken wire fence at the end of the road. They had their bikes leaned against a huge pine tree that had dropped a blanket of rust-brown needles on the ground. They looked up when I got closer but then went back to what they were doing, pretending not to notice me.

"Got a firecracker?" I asked. They looked at me quickly.

"No, sir." The small one snapped out. The bigger one had something behind his back.

"I got a match." I didn't, but I just felt like saying it.

"So?" He lowered his small hands; they were filled with sparklers.

"What's on the other side of that fence?" I stood next to their bikes, about ten feet from the fence. There was a lot of trees, too dense to see what was on the other side.

"A creek," one said. "Some more trailers," said the other.

There was a gap in the fence, and a large cement post, like the base of a small monument. I cut through the gap and walked down a path. It sloped downward. It was cooler under the trees. I saw the sky through the canopy of branches and leaves. A raccoon scurried up a trunk.

I saw a lawn chair in a little depression near a pile of ashes and burnt branches that must have once been a bonfire. I sat down and just kind of let my weight sink into it, and I looked around, felt dizzy, and relaxed. I didn't see the creek the kids had mentioned.

The area must have been a place for vagrants or teenagers who wanted to smoke cigarettes and drink beer. Same with the vagrants. There were a few of them who wandered around the trailer park. They dug through trash cans and hung out. Generally, they didn't cause any trouble.

I heard the two kids by the fence trying to light their sparklers.

Diamond Kennel wasn't my problem. I wasn't sure it ever had been. I was more a part of it than part of the solution. That's what plagued me. John had fired me because of body tour, and he knew about the body tour because of Dr. Fielding. And why would Dr. Fielding tell John about that? Fielding had put himself at risk. He had Cal in a cage in his hospital. He knew he would see me again. I was missing a piece. That much was obvious. Fielding must have had a motive, and the motive must have been substantial enough, at least in his mind, to put his own career at risk.

The two brown kids stumbled down the trail with two lit sparklers. In the daylight the sparklers didn't look too bright, but I heard them fizzle, and the kids were laughing and smiling. They stopped near the edge of the trail to let me see them. They stood together on the sloping path and waved the sparklers in the air.

I had taken my truck from Greenhorns to Animal Control, called a taxi, and emptied out the truck while I waited. I didn't say good-bye to Molly. Marvin Bell had been out front cleaning mud off the tires of his truck. He had waved and asked how I was doing in that slow, Southern accent he had, and I had said fine, then turned away. He saw me get in the cab and leave my truck.

It was hard to leave that truck. I had spent so much time inside of it. I knew it well, depended on it. When I rode away in the taxi, I felt like someone had died. I smoked a cigar in the back while the cabbie played disco music on an 8-track. I had thought about going to get Cal first, but then decided not to because he was fine and I didn't want to see Fielding so soon. I didn't want to face him for the last time and not have the courage to ask him why he had taken my job.

As I sat in the lawn chair beneath the trees and the two kids went back up the trail, I tried to think of a reason. I looked back on all that had happened between Dr. Fielding and me. Maybe he thought I'd do something about the track, about the testosterone, but then why would he fear me? I had taken his money, placed the bet, and profited from it. I was a willing participant. And if he was worried about my role as an Animal Control officer, the worst thing in the world he could have done was piss me off. How would he know that I'd be fired? And if I hadn't, I would have gone after him. Surely, he had thought of that.

I searched the kitchen cabinets for food: yellow rice, tuna fish, and two bags of dry beans. The beans would take too long to cook, so I started the rice in a pot of water on the gas stove. I stripped and took a shower while the rice was cooking. I shaved, then dressed in my green slacks, green short-sleeve shirt, and black boots. Then I ate the rice while looking up Dr. Julius Gant in the phone book.

I figured that he would be a good place to start. He had phoned in the complaint that sent me to Diamond Kennel. I hoped John would appreciate the information. I wanted my job back. And I thought that maybe, when the Holton case was over, he would be ready to take me, body tour or not.

I had met Julius Gant when Kelly Tipp, another Animal Control officer, had rescued four nighthawks from a pack of kids. Some people called them whipporwills. Nighthawks had feathers like owls and long, rubbery eyelashes. They slept in the daytime, usually on the sides of hills in mounds of thick grass. At night, they hunted insects, using their large mouths like nets. The kids had hunted them. Fortunately one of the mothers found them and called Animal Control.

Kelly Tipp didn't know where to take them. John and Molly had left for lunch, so she called me on the mobile phone. Gant had done some wildlife work before, so I gave Kelly directions and met her there. He had taken the birds, no charge. We talked briefly. Actually, Gant lectured. He was the type of person who thought everybody was interested in what he had to say about bird sonar or the cellular make-up of turtles. Kelly got buzzed on her mobile phone while Gant was talking, and she got out. I hadn't been as lucky.

I found his number, took the book to the bedroom and called. I made an appointment for 1:45. I told the receptionist I was bringing my dog in for a heartworm exam.

Then I called a taxi. It was the same cabbie who played the disco music. He picked me up in the driveway of the trailer, and I told him to drive to the Barnett Bank, and wait outside. It was a small bank, with only one teller sitting on a stool behind a fake marble counter. Her blonde, almost orange, head of hair looked electric against all the black furniture and dark wallpaper. I walked up to the counter and filled out a withdrawal slip for $2,000. I helped myself to a handful of peppermints in a glass jar while she tapped the keys on her computer.

I took most of the money in hundred-dollar bills, some twenties and tens. I folded the wad and wrapped a rubber band around it, then put it in my front right pocket. The teller watched me curiously. I'm sure she thought I was working because I was in uniform, and she must have wondered what I would need that much money for.

I gave the cabbie directions to a used car lot about a mile from the bank. It was one of those we-finance-anyone places, called Rooney's Clean and Used. They had all the hoods opened on the autos in front of the lot. I supposed that made them look honest. I paid the cabbie and stood outside on the dry cedar chips that covered the lot. Finally, a salesman came out of the single-wide trailer at the back of the lot. He wore a short-sleeved, sky blue oxford, cheap sunglasses and what looked like golfing shoes. He had a ruddy, alcoholic complexion. We shook hands.

I pointed to a black minicab in a row of trucks under two palm trees held up with two-by-fours. It was a Chevy Luv with extra-wide rear tires. It had 800.00 written in white soap across the windshield. I offered the salesman six hundred cash, and he didn't look at all surprised.

"You want to wait while I get the title?"

The key was inside the truck. I got in and sat down. The interior was vinyl, made to look like leather. It was tan, and the truck smelled like cigarettes. The dashboard was cracked, and there was a faded Christmas tree hanging from the rearview mirror.

The salesman came back with the title in hand. I gave him the money. He told me to go easy on the clutch—after the cash was tucked in his back pocket.

I drove my truck to Gant's. I tried to formulate a plan, a way to approach the topic of the phone call and Dr. Fielding, but I couldn't think of anything other than asking him straight out. I could use my uniform a little, though I was sure Gant wouldn't scare. He knew I couldn't touch him, even if I really had something to touch him with.

Besides, I was looking for allies, not enemies.

Dr. Julius Gant's hospital was right next to a fire station. He had a large blue sign facing the road with his name in block letters across the top: Julius Gant, DVM. Below that it said: X-Rays, Surgery, Specializing in Exotics and Wildlife Rehabilitation.

There were two cars in the front parking lot, a black Mercedes and an old Honda hatchback. I parked near the Honda, stubbed my cigar out, and straightened my shirt. I had brought my clipboard along for the sake of image. I walked in the front door, and it was like walking into a cave. Gant had a fish tank in the middle of the reception area, about thirty gallons. Three parrot fish circled around a nice reef, lots of air bubbles climbed up the sides of the glass. The walls of the clinic were dark, made of this plastic stuff that looked like rock. There were wooden benches bolted into the fake rock wall. A woman wearing a curly wig and a fancy dress sat on one of the benches. She held a white poodle on the end of a short leash. I nodded to her when I walked in.

The receptionist's desk was tall and long, like a bar. The receptionist looked down at me when I walked up to it.

"Hello." She shuffled papers.

"Good afternoon. May I see Dr. Gant, please?"

"Well," she looked at her calendar, "he's got an appointment at 1:45. Do you want to wait?"

"It won't take too long. Maybe I could talk to him till your client arrives."

She considered me a moment, then flipped her long, brown hair across her right shoulder and smiled.

"OK," she said.

Of course, I knew her appointment would never show up, and so I had ample time to loosen up Dr. Gant and find out what I could. She took me down a hallway that was covered with posters of wildlife. We went through a door marked Employees Only, and I saw Dr. Gant sitting on a stool, reading a magazine, and eating from a bowl. He looked up and had a string of pasta hanging from his mouth. He was a short man with a bald spot and round, wire-rimmed glasses, in green surgical scrubs and dirty white tennis shoes. He had a front pocket full of pens, and a stethoscope around his neck.

"I'm Dr. Gant. Can I help you?" He left his pasta on the X-ray table and stood up. He had a concerned look on his face, as if something had gone wrong.

"Nice to meet you again, Doctor." I shook his hand.

"I've met you before? Oh, I guess I have." He took the stethoscope from around his neck and set it on the counter where there were rows of pill bottles.

"I brought you a few nighthawks, about a year ago."

"I think I remember. What can I do for the county now?"

"Is there someplace we can talk?"

"Well, sure. How about talking while I feed the owls? I have three screech owls. Have you ever fed them?"

"No." I said. I had never fed screech owls.

Dr. Gant opened a freezer door and took out a Tupperware cube. He set the cube on the counter and cracked open the lid.

"Come on." He walked around a corner by the X-ray machine. We emerged in front of his office. He went inside and sat behind the desk, which faced the wall. I sat in a leather chair next to the desk. He had his diplomas on the wall, one from the University of Florida, and another from Pennsylvania. There was a picture of two young boys in front of a swing set, framed in chrome on the corner of his desk. Dr. Gant folded his hands on his stomach and sighed. "We have to let them thaw out a little." He looked over the tops of his glasses.

I didn't understand, and he must have noticed the look on my face because he told me that there were crickets in the Tupperware cube. When they thawed out, they came back to life, he said. I didn't quite believe it, but was interested in checking it out.

"The county sent me here, Dr. Gant." I said politely, and set my clipboard on my lap.

"On official business, huh? I'm sorry. Just a little joke. I'm part German you know." He chuckled to himself.

I didn't know what being German had to do with it. "I'd like to know a little more about the complaint you phoned in about Diamond Kennel."

"Did you send people there?" He sat up, interested.

"I went there. I'm in charge of the investigation."

"Good, so there's an investigation at least. Did you see anything? Well, I guess you did."

"I saw the kennel, and a supply of testosterone, just like you said. I also saw a local veterinarian and heard something about a farm nearby."

"You didn't see the farm?" His voice rose in genuine alarm.

"No, but I've heard about it."

"Well, that's the problem. You've got to see the farm to understand. Do you know what those greyhound people do to the dogs? It makes me sick."

"I'd like to try and stop it," I said.

"Would you?" He perked an eyebrow.

"You'll have to help me."

"What is it you want to know?"

"Well, there's a lot of things that I'm confused about."

"The crickets." He jumped from his chair and disappeared through the office door.

I followed him back to the treatment room. The lid to the Tupperware cube had opened more when it thawed.

"Who was the veterinarian you saw at Diamond Kennel?" He cracked the lid open slightly more.

The owls were in a bird cage on another counter near stacks of larger aluminum cages. There were two cats, each in a cage, wrapped in towels. Their eyes were moist and dreamy. Dr. Gant spooned the crickets into the cage where the three Screech owls, pale, hideous wads of wrinkled skin, huddled in the back of the birdcage.

"Is it important?"

Dr. Gant laughed. "Hell, yes, it's important. OK, I'll tell you that it was Dr. Fielding. Surprised? Well, you should know that Dr. Fielding owns that farm, that kennel, those dogs, and a whole lot more."

As soon as Dr. Gant had closed the door to the birdcage, the three screech owls picked at any grasshopper that jumped by them. Dr. Gant studied them for a minute, then used a hemostat, snipped a grasshopper, and shoved it into the mouth of an owl.

Things made a lot more sense if Dr. Fielding owned Diamond Kennel. Like Cathy for one. Had she known Dr. Fielding was her boss?

Of course she did. She had also chosen not to tell me.

"How do you know this, Dr. Gant?" I stepped back as he closed the door to the birdcage.

"It's not a secret." He wiped his hands on the front of his scrub shirt.

"It's not common knowledge, either."

"I don't know how to explain. You should know this, anyway. The greyhounds, the track, the trainers, all of it is so secretive when you try and look a little closer. It's like they operate under a rock or under a screen." He fanned his hands in the air to show me. "I've always supposed it was the state. You know taxes on gambling and all that. They must make millions."

"Maybe billions."

"Maybe. So I would say that nothing the greyhounders do is common knowledge, really."

We walked back to his office. He offered me a cup of coffee, and we talked about business, nighthawks. Dr. Gant told me that he had no real power. That if he put pressure on Dr. Fielding to upgrade the condition of his greyhound-breeding farm, he would lose clients, money, and the cooperation of other local vets. Dr. Fielding was an old boy, he explained. Fielding knew many people, had many clients, had done many wonderful things. Dr. Gant was young, new. He'd made the call to Animal Control, but no more. He wasn't willing to sacrifice everything he had worked for to stop one farm, and one group of greyhounders. It was more important for him to continue doing what he was capable of doing.

I finished my coffee and thanked him. He had told me a lot more than I had expected to hear. The question was, what was I going to do with it? Dr. Gant walked me to the front door. The woman with the wig and the poodle was still waiting by the fish tank.

It was a hot day. The firemen next door had their trucks on the driveway and were washing them down. I was surprised by my truck in the parking lot. When I had first looked at it, I didn't realize it was mine. I had expected to see my orange-and-white Animal Control truck out there. I got inside the Luv, started it, and tried the air conditioning. It just blew warm, wet air into the cab. Maybe I'd get it fixed when it was all over.

Chapter 9

There were two greyhounds in the outside cage at the side of Dr. Fielding's hospital. They both were black and kind of small. I parked next to a blue van with tinted windows and a long CB antennae.

I walked around the cage to a glass door with slabs of wood across it. The two small greyhounds followed like children from inside their cage. Cal saw me. He jumped up in his cage, his nails scratching on the aluminum flooring. I went over to him and opened the cage door. He hopped out and let his tail thump and wag. He sniffed and coughed while I petted his head and his chest. His fur was shaved around his ribs on both sides.

It would have been the easiest thing in the world to slip out the door, put Cal in the truck, and drive home, but I knew I couldn't do it. And it wasn't because Dr. Fielding would know that I had taken Cal. It was something else. I had trusted him. I had even let myself be guided by his orders at the track and at Diamond Kennel.

I took a blue choker off a hook near the trash compactor and passed it over Cal's head. He didn't fight. He must have been so glad to be getting out of there that he didn't mind the leash. I walked up the long hallway with Cal. I realized that it was probably the last time I'd ever see Dr. Fielding's hospital. Now why should that make me sad? Maybe it was the fact that everything seemed to start and stop in that hallway. The place was like a goddamn church.

Dr. Fielding's voice rose from his office. I stopped and pushed Cal's rump down so he would sit. I put my hand on his ears to keep him quiet. Dr. Fielding was arguing with two other men. They sounded calm and uninterested in the fact that Dr. Fielding wanted more money than they seemed able to give.

One of the strangers said, "We've got to get driving."

Then Dr. Fielding: "We have a contract."

"Not any contract you could sue over." The other stranger said.

After that the office was quiet. I took Cal back down the hallway, out the door, and into the Luv. I picked him up and put him in the seat, then rolled the window down halfway. I took a pen from my pocket, and walked around the back of the truck to see the van's license plate.

It was a university plate. The state university was in Satchoolee, about two hundred miles from Palm County. I wrote the plate number on a scrap of paper and tucked it in my pocket. I felt I had discovered something valuable. Then the two strangers came out the back door. I stood at the back of my truck, in uniform, and the first one, who was wearing white coveralls and looked like a weightlifter, dropped his jaw. He stared, and the second stranger bumped into his back on the way out the door. The second man pushed him out of the way while herding the two greyhounds together. The weightlifter helped him. The second man wore a tie, black loafers and plastic sunglasses. He was heavy, and rings of sweat soaked through his dress shirt.

I watched them gather the two scared greyhounds with blue choker leashes and lead them to the gate door. I saw Dr. Fielding staring out from the glass in the back door. I couldn't tell if he was watching me. The glass had wire mesh in it, and the sun was bright, but I knew he saw me. What else could he see?

Cal growled from inside the Luv as the two men pulled the greyhounds toward the blue van. I stepped into their path, dropped my arms to my sides. "Hello, gentlemen."

The man wearing the tie pushed his sunglasses up and coughed. Sweat dripped from his moustache to his lip. "Can I help you?"

"Where are you going with those dogs?"

"I don't see how that's your concern."

"I'm making it my concern right now."

The weightlifter handed his leash to the other man, then stepped forward.

The man wearing the tie laughed uneasily. "Animal Control don't have shit to do with this, buddy. Just let me go on."

From the corner of my eye, I saw the back door swing open, and I knew it was Dr. Fielding. The sun sparked across his glasses as he walked into the hot, black parking lot where we stood. The greyhounds started pacing. Their paws were getting burned on the pavement.

"Legget!" Dr. Fielding yelled. It was a tone I had never heard from him. Anger cut at the edge of it. "Step away!" he yelled again.

"I can't do that, Doc."

"He's not a dog catcher anymore." Dr. Fielding told the two men.

"Bullshit," one said.

"It's true," Dr. Fielding said pleadingly.

The weightlifter smiled.

"You don't know that for a fact, Doc, though you tried damned hard to make it one."

"The Lord giveth and the Lord taketh away," he said.

Dr. Fielding stood next to the man wearing the tie. He reached down and petted the smaller greyhound. It wagged its tail. Dr. Fielding then knelt next to the dog and kissed it on the face, while the dog licked his mouth. "They're beautiful dogs, Legget. Loyal in every way. They trust us completely. Could you trust me that much?" His voice trailed off.

"How much do you get for them? Jesus, Doc, I thought you cared about these animals."

"That's not what I was hoping you'd say, Legget," Dr. Fielding whispered.

As I strained to hear Dr. Fielding, the weightlifter lunged, grabbed me under both arms, and pushed. I saw only his young, round face and the overpass behind it closing in. After that, I was confused by sound and red flashes, a heaviness in my chest and head. I knew he had me on the ground, and I saw Cal barking in the front seat, lunging toward the window, his teeth wet and white behind the glass, but I couldn't hear him. The weightlifter pounded the back of my head, and I tried to fight back, but each time I did, the blows came harder, so I stopped, went slack, my cheek pressed hard against the gravelly pavement. I heard Dr. Fielding behind me, tasted spit or blood in my mouth, something warm and thick anyway. It was hot. I felt pain, but also a strong compulsion to get Cal. I couldn't leave him in the truck. I was thinking, if I go unconscious, Cal will get heat stroke. I tried to stay awake, but it was heavy. My head was heavy and warm and moist.

When I did wake up, I knew right away I was in Dr. Fielding's office because I opened my eyes and saw the glass jar with the water puppy inside, all yellow and wrinkled and bloated on his desk in front of me. I lay on the couch. There was no one else in the room, and I didn't know how long I'd been there.

I got up from the couch and walked down the hallway toward the freezer. There was a white cat with blue eyes and a one-legged German shepherd in cages, but no Cal. His cage had been cleaned out and layered with newspaper. It was still light outside. I saw the light coming in from the glass window in the door. My face was swollen. I could feel it as if water had been pumped behind my skin. My eyes watered, and I felt dizzy.

Outside, I saw the Luv and stumbled to it, looked inside, but Cal wasn't there. The two black greyhounds were gone. Fielding had sold them to the university for medical research. There was no other explanation.

Inside again, I was thankful for the air conditioning. Fielding must be with a client. I searched the back of his hospital once more for Cal, but didn't find anything except sacks of food, paper towels, empty IV bottles, and venosets, and blankets, and towels. His clinic had once been a house.

The floors were cement. They had once been blue, but then they were cold gray and silver in the middle where people walked all the time. There were chips of blue near the walls. The walls were made of cinder block. I saw the lines where the blocks sat one on top of the other. The lines blurred together in the geometry. The large white freezer was a rectangular bulk crowding the rear of the hallway. It hummed, the way engines hum. Next to it a new, shiny washer and dryer.

Some of the walls had been painted, some not, which made the back look something like a garage. Yellow here, dingy white with green scratches where the oxygen tanks were braced against it and chafing. The German shepherd watched me walk around. A rusty chain hung from a two-by-four in the ceiling. Beyond it, the darkness of the roof, and crawl space. The place smelled like alcohol, piss, and animal fur. But after a while, it smelled normal, and everything else was ripe and alive. Normal smells were not normal.

I bent over the bathtub which was propped about two and a half feet above the floor. It had been built that way to wash the animals. I washed my hands and face with a strong, red soap that smelled like apples. When I touched my face I felt the bruises, a bad one under my right eye, one on each cheek, and then a real bad one in the middle of my throat.

I passed his office and peeked in. The lights were off, and I sensed no movement from inside. Beyond the X-ray machine, which had balls of dust and hair accumulating underneath, I heard Dr. Fielding. He was in the front of the hospital. It sounded like he was talking to a client. His voice was steady, confident, the voice of a doctor who knew everything. They all seemed to know everything, and I wondered why that was.

I waited in the treatment room. There was a chrome tub with a tubular, steel rack set on top of it in the middle of the floor. To my right were three small cages one on top of the other. Behind me, a counter and shelves, a sink that operated with a foot pedal. In the sink, a steel tray filled with a milky, blue fluid, and in the fluid were tools: a hemostat, empty syringe casings, and something that looked like pliers. The shelves were filled with bottles, injectables, many colors on the labels, and long words. One bottle had a needle stuck into the rubber stopper.

Fielding opened the door out of the examination room and looked up the hallway at me. He raised his hand but didn't say anything. He dropped a thick file on the counter near a microscope and opened a cabinet, appearing to study the rows of pill bottles and tonics arranged inside. His technician came out of the room, took the file, and spread it open on the counter. She set up some test in a clear, plastic tube while Dr. Fielding pulled the microscope away from the wall and adjusted the knobs.

I started to walk up the hall, but then he raised his hands again and headed toward the treatment room. It was hard to look at him.

He leaned against the stack of cages. When his shoulder pressed into the side of a cage, they rolled and he almost toppled it. I started to help him but stopped myself. Why did I want to help him? He looked old, not the man I had thought him to be. He had performed no miracles, nor would he ever. He was possessed by greed and power, and I pitied him. As we both stood in the treatment room, the awkward, almost tangible silence between us growing slowly, I felt no anger. But I also knew I would break him. It was all I could do.

He walked past me and I didn't stop him. His technician came up from the hallway, said hello, and told me Cal was up front near the window. I went up there alone and found Cal. He was calm and wagged his tail slowly when I called him. It was hot in the front of the clinic because of the large window. Cal followed me to the back.

Fielding was in his office again with the television on. I went inside as he was pouring whiskey into a plastic cup. He had a little tray on the cushion next to him with a vial of yellow medicine and a small syringe like a diabetic used. "I'm sorry about what happened, Legget. I found your little note."

"I could have you arrested."

"I know."

"What note?" I tried to play dumb.

He went to the sink, poured water from the tap into the cup, then lifted his prescription pad from his smock. "The one Cathy wrote to you on this pad. I saw her. She's pretty, but she isn't too smart."

He showed me the page where he'd rubbed a pencil and a copy of the whole note she'd written was right there. He went back to the couch, put his drink down and put the tray on his lap. He had another vial of something dark in his pocket and took it out, then pulled some out with the syringe. Then he mixed the dark stuff with a little of the yellow and flicked the syringe with his finger.

I guessed the note was why he'd told John about body tour. A way to cover his ass. When he stuck that syringe tip into the vein in his arm, I thought I was dreaming. But there it was. He'd done it right in front of me. I thought things weren't real, that I was dreaming all this. Cal had strayed far down the hall, and I went to get him back. As I passed, the German shepherd growled. It stood in the cage and pushed against the wire door. The dog had only three legs. Cal sat and watched the shepherd growl.

I checked my keys and returned to Fielding's office. He was sitting on the couch watching a game show. The TV was very loud.

"What was that shit?"

He looked away from the TV. His eyes were heavy and mellow. "Crystal K," he said and turned back like it was nothing.

I was standing behind him in the open doorway, and something happened inside me. I walked to the TV, grabbed the back of it and flung it from the stand.

There was a great crash of glass and bright sparks. Fielding shielded his face with his arms, spilling the drink and losing his glasses. I watched the television explode as if it were in slow motion. Fielding balled up on the couch as if I were about to attack him. Then I left his clinic with my dog.

When I was piling Cal into the truck, Fielding appeared behind the fence, leaned into it heavily and stared at me.

"I guess this means we're not on friendly terms anymore," he said as I opened my door.

"Guess not, Doc."

"I would have helped you, Legget."

"Yeah," I said and slammed the door.

* * *

I wasn't sure if Cathy would be home, and I was worried that my timing would be bad. But I was compelled to find her. There was a point where I felt myself blurring at the edges, disappearing into what surrounded me, and I needed an ally. Cathy, I believed, was all I had. I hadn't thought of myself as needing a woman in quite the way I felt as I drove the truck through the afternoon traffic. The people in the cars and trucks around me were alone and looked unhappy. They looked pale and wooden behind the glass. I had thought I was different.

The Luv sputtered after the day's hard driving, and the clutch pedal stuck to the floor. It was a hot day, and there was much traffic. I stopped at a 7-Eleven for Sweets and bought four. I was still in uniform, and hoped that I didn't run into Saul Tilly, who worked the part of town that Cathy lived in. But strangely, the dog catchers were rarely seen. I had people tell me before that they didn't even know we existed. They had never spotted our trucks on the streets. And I supposed if you weren't looking for a dog catcher, one would never appear.

I had no idea whether Cathy owned a car or not. I had never asked. A stray cat wandered through the shrubs, rubbing his dirty orange fur against a cracked drainpipe. I stopped to try and pet him, but he bolted off. I took the stairs to her apartment, took a deep breath, then knocked softly. I didn't know what to expect. The time we had spent together seemed distant, a world away.

I heard her shuffling inside the apartment. She opened the door, blocking Slick with her foot. Her eyes were wide, honest, with a touch of darkness around the edges. Her hair looked plain but clean. She hadn't styled it, just pulled it back away from her face. It gave me a sore spot in my chest for her. I ached with the scent and presence of her.

I felt cold air rush out of her open door, then smelled her perfume, and the way her apartment smelled, like dog and oranges and old coffee. There was an open magazine on the edge of the couch. The television was on, and a sweating glass of orange or fruit juice was on the coffee table. Cathy let me inside; I sat on a square, green chair with a matching ottoman. She turned down the volume of the television, then sat on the couch, crossing one leg beneath the other. Slick jumped onto the couch next to her, and she settled in.

"Are you waiting for a call?" I pointed to the telephone.

"Not really," she shrugged. "What happened to your face?"

Slick nosed her magazine off the couch, trying to get closer to her.

"Want something to drink?"

"Yes. But I can get it. I had an unhappy customer today. I'd like to forget about it."

There was coffee in an electric percolator on the counter, but it looked muddy. There were a few dirty dishes in the sink, an empty carton of half-and-half toppled on the counter, and an open bag of sugar. I opened her refrigerator and was surprised to find it pretty empty. I checked the freezer for ice cubes. There were trays in a rack on the left side.

I filled a plastic cup from the tap, and dropped a few cubes in. Slick came in to see what I was doing. Cathy had her back to me. Her hair was rolled and set on her right shoulder; her neck was bare and long. The cords on each side were dotted with tiny freckles. Her shirt curled up and puckered when she turned the pages of the magazine. I drank the water, stood in the kitchen and stared at her back. She lifted her leg out from underneath her and stretched it out on the coffee table. A lean, freckled, soft leg with a small knee and long toes.

I drank my water, took a deep breath. Slick nudged against my leg, so I dumped my ice cubes in his water bowl. I glanced up, and she was smiling, a pleased smile that warmed me inside. I noticed a dent in the tip of her nose, just a small groove that made her face light up and section off like a drawing or a painting maybe. Her face had detail. She was very brown, hair and eyes and freckles. Warm and brown and smiling at me.

I walked back to the living room, set my glass on her coffee table, and petted Slick, who had followed me from the kitchen.

"Why aren't you working today?" I asked.

"I'll go in later. When it's feeding time." She put her magazine down. A puzzled, quizzical look appeared on her face.

"Sit over here, Legget." She pointed toward the couch. "Come on." She patted the seat.

I went to the couch. When I sat down a great weight sunk into it. Cathy stood. "I'll be right back."

She returned with a clear bottle and cotton. She sat next to me. "Close your eyes," she said.

I closed my eyes. I felt her fingers on my face. The cotton was wet and smelled like rain.

"Witch hazel," she said, rubbing it around the bruises on my neck.

"It feels good, Cath."

"Just relax." She stopped.

A moment later, her hands pulled at the button of my pants. I kept my eyes closed as long as I could, then helped her. Her body was warm. She was tender, which made me feel the same. We shut Slick out of the bedroom and went to the bed.

Chapter 10

In the morning we found nothing in Cathy's refrigerator, so she volunteered to go to the grocery store if she could borrow my truck. She wanted to go on her own for some reason, and I didn't argue. After the door clicked shut behind her, Slick gave me a look. Maybe he was weighing the idea of me being where only Cathy had been before. It was cool in the apartment. I flicked on the television and sat on the couch where Cathy had just been sitting, and the smell of her was strong there.

I couldn't sit still. I kept thinking about Fielding, so I wandered back to the bedroom. It was darker inside because we had draped a blue sheet over the window. Slick watched me walk in like a snoop, and I felt guilty. I had that strange moment when you think an animal might know more than it should, and it just hit me how I'd made love again to this woman I hardly knew. The blue satin comforter was tossed aside where we had left it, the pillows bunched on her side.

Stepping closer, I noticed her hair on one pillow. I reached out and brushed it off. I dragged my fingers across the sheets, just under the edge of the comforter, and it was warm inside where she had tucked her legs and arms in last night. Behind me, there was a white dresser with a mirror leaned on the top and an assortment of bottles, boxes, belts, and jewelry. I picked up the perfume bottles and smelled, looking for the oranges she liked to wear. I put them back where I found them, touched some of her jewelry. There was nothing expensive. Brown elephant earrings, a sterling silver bracelet with a heart charm and the initials SKU on the face.

Taped to the mirror was a single photograph of Cathy standing in front of a small shack with loose boards and new, vanilla-colored planks stacked by it. The photo didn't seem that old, but she looked younger. There were woods behind the shack. Tall pine, oak. It didn't look like Diamond Kennel, and some of the trees were strange. They were shorter than the oaks, with all their branches growing almost straight up.

She came in just a few moments later with two grocery bags, one under each arm. She dropped my keys on the couch, kicked the door shut from behind, then dropped the bags on the kitchen counter.

We unloaded the bags. She had bought pickles soaked in garlic water, ham, sliced muenster cheese, potato chips, and pineapple juice. She took mustard and bread from a cabinet. I arranged the groceries on the counter, and Cathy excused herself to the bedroom.

She came out of her bedroom with her backpack, a loose white tank top, red shorts, and a black baseball cap with a white *S* above the bill. She had tied her hair into a ponytail and run the tail through a hole in the cap. She dropped her backpack by the door, went to the kitchen and started packing up the food. She had a picnic basket with colored, plastic plates that matched the forks, spoons and cups. They attached to clips on the inside flap of the basket. She wrapped the food in bags and paper towels, poured the juice into a thermos and added a few ice cubes. I tried to help, but she was quick and had a clear purpose.

I poured Slick some fresh water and Cathy said a long good-bye, then we trudged out the door toward my truck. I climbed in the driver's side and pushed open the door for her.

Cathy gave directions. I drove us through town, then off through a large suburban development called Timber Lanes. She guided me to a dirt road at the back of the complex, where there were empty trucks and trailers for the construction crew.

"Are you sure?" I slowed.

"This brings back memories," she said with pursed lips. I pulled onto the dirt road and started bouncing in the seat when we rolled over the dirt and rocks and dips. At first, the road was open and clear. The trees had been sliced down to make way for more houses. But after we drove about five minutes, the trees reappeared with silver moss and dead branches. There were pools of water in holes, and saw grass. To my right, through clumps of cattails and tall lemon grass, a wild pond. The surface was still, and there were no cuts along the shore for boats to get in.

It was getting hot and sticky in the truck. Dragonflies and gnats and other bugs started to smack against the windshield and buzz through the open windows. I looked over at Cathy. She didn't look back, but watched the road as if she were looking for a street sign to appear from behind the skeleton of a dead tree.

I had to stop the truck because the road narrowed. Cathy packed up our things and jumped out. I followed her onto a trail that started at the side of the road. The pond was on our right, through a wall of strong-smelling weeds and cattails—the kind of smell that builds up from heat and still water and plants.

"Thanks for letting me drag you out here, Legget." Cathy swatted at a horsefly. "I didn't want to come alone."

"I wish you'd told me we were going on safari," I said.

"I haven't been here in a while. Sorry."

Cathy had strong legs, a pink blemish on the back of her right thigh. Her hair almost reached the small of her back. It came out of her baseball cap in one long tube. A shine of sweat had formed on the backs of her arms.

"Want me to carry that basket, Cath?"

"I got it," she said over her shoulder.

We rounded a small hill of dirt and dark sand. A few rocks wedged into the bottom, then a sloping track down the middle. I wondered if I'd get the chance to find out why all this was happening. I saw motorcycle treads along the spine of the hill. We walked around the little hill, and the pond was out of sight. The ground was harder, and I started to see little patches of grass.

"OK." Cathy stopped, then turned around. "We've got to climb a little. It looks smaller than I remember."

"Jesus."

"Quite an adventure, huh?"

"Look Cath. I've come this far. Maybe you could tell me ..."

She turned around and nodded, looked me in the eye, like she had something heavy on her mind. "OK. I know this place. I've been thinking a lot. About us. I used to come here when I was younger. Me and Sam." She put down the basket, lifted a rock, and tossed it over the hill. I heard it thunk into the water.

"You could carry the basket now," she said.

I lifted the basket. Cathy poked through a few bushes in front of us. She found the spot she was looking for and waved me over. As I walked closer, she disappeared. I sped up and stood where she'd been, looked in. There was a small footpath running downward through the thick bush. It was visible about ten feet, then it darkened as the bush crept overhead and blocked out the sun. It looked like a tunnel. The air that blew up from the tunnel felt cooler and smelled like mint. "Cath?" No answer.

I stepped onto the path and almost stumbled because it was steeper than it looked. I shimmied down after her, smacking into branches and leaves as I fell deeper into it. I thought of the times I had done things like that while hunting for a dog or a raccoon. There were areas like it all around the county, many of them populated with wild dogs. People drove their pets there, then dumped them. The animals survived off trash, became scavengers.

The path turned right. I ducked under a heavy palm frond that stuck out. The tunnel ended. There were clumps of palm bushes spread over a field of tall grass. Cathy stood about ten feet away next to a shack. She peered into a broken window.

"Come on!" She scooped the air with her arm.

The shack was framed with pine and oak and palm. I looked back toward the tunnel I had descended through and could see the top of the ridge, but the tunnel was gone. I saw only the tops of the bush. We had come down the small ridge and stood at the edge of what I imagined was a field. I couldn't see far enough through the trees to know exactly. Cathy walked over and took the basket.

"What do you think?" She took my hand and tugged me closer. "Isn't this great?" She pushed open the door of the shack.

It was one room. Strings of sunlight poked through the walls over a rusted bed frame in one corner, a chrome tub that had turned to an emerald green, a stack of wooden egg crates, and a pile of magazines. I didn't think it was so great. Cathy sat on one of the egg crates, kicked another out for me. She put the basket between our seats, adjusted her hat and looked around, smiling.

"Why did you and Sam come here?" I asked, then tested the sturdiness of the crate, sat down.

Cathy squinted and seemed to look through me. Cryptic. "I told you we lived nearby."

"It sure is strange. I feel like I've traveled to another country."

"That's why I like it. I'm afraid it won't be like this forever. As soon as all those houses are sold, they'll start building more over here."

"I'm surprised it's been here this long."

"I'm sure there are kids in Timber Lane that know of it, but they don't do anything more than drink beer or smoke pot, or maybe screw." She looked at the bed frame. There were a few empty beer bottles underneath, and cigarette butts.

Cathy unpacked the basket and started putting the sandwiches together.

"We didn't have it easy, you know. I'm not saying I'm special. Lots of kids have parents that—" she looked up at me and pretended she was tipping back a bottle. I got the idea. "That's how we got into greyhounds," she said and laughed a little. "Beer."

"How's that?" I asked.

"Well, when the dogs were in town, my father would take us to the track, which was a lot better than the off season. Then he'd go to a titty bar and leave us in a McDonalds across the street all day. The track was better. Bigger, a lot more to see. I think the beer was cheaper too. Fifty cents a draft, and he could drink all day in the shade of the bleachers."

She was saying it like a joke, but it wasn't. I heard how her voice cracked at the edges.

"So that's how Sam learned to train the dogs?"

"I suppose that's how it started. When he had to go to work he was fifteen, maybe fourteen. He went right to the track. They knew him. One of the old dog men took him in. It didn't matter that he knew nothing about the dogs."

"And you?"

"Sam tried to keep me from working, but leaving me alone with the old man was worse. So when I was sixteen, Sam fixed it up. He was running the dogs by then."

"So what's this place got to do with it?"

She handed me a sandwich, but I wasn't hungry.

"Go on," she said, trying to get me to eat. "Me and Sam would come here when things got hard. You know a drunk goes through these waves of acting crazy; then everything is calm, then back to crazy. Jesus, I don't want to say it."

"You don't have to, Cath. I understand. Lot of people like that, where I come from." I tried to touch her wrist, but she pulled away. "So you and Sam came here because it was safe. Just someplace you guys stumbled on to."

"Yeah. Would you mind? This is all coming back so hard, Legget."

She nodded like she wanted to be alone.

So I went outside, where it was warm and moist. I felt sheltered by the ridge and the wall of trees behind the shack. I walked a ways through the grass and realized I was in a sort of bowl with one low side. The only way out was back up the ridge or through the trees. I peeked through and saw that the trees were only fifty or so feet deep, and more of the same swampy landscape was on the other side.

Cathy came out of the shack with a sandwich in each hand. I'd left mine inside. I met her halfway and took one. She had already eaten some of hers. We sat down in the grass under the shade of one of the peeling trees.

"Are these sycamores?"

"I think so,"

"Did anyone live here?"

"I don't know."

"You had to come here often?"

"When he was drunk and looking for something to do."

"That was often enough, I imagine."

"Funny we should sit here," she said and slapped her hands clean. "I believe this is exactly where I was when he found us. He scared me to death. Sam was with me. We'd skipped school together; we did everything together. He came over the ridge there and I saw him." She pointed to a chunk of grass that looked no different than the rest.

"We watched him, I don't know, ten minutes. Just standing there, swaying a little, like a ghost. I guess the school had called him. I don't know. Sam said to just pretend he wasn't there and put a monkey wrench in his back pocket, one of those heavy wrenches, and I knew it was going to be serious. He gets that way. God, I remember him just standing up there drunk, like we couldn't see him. You don't know what a man like that is thinking. He ignored us until Sam started throwing pebbles. He even ignored that, but one hit him right in the chest, and I remember seeing him wince, not a noise, but physically, you know, his body kind of tensed up and weakened. Well, that scared the shit out of me, but Sam laughed."

She handed me the rest of her sandwich which I took and ate slowly. She looked around as if seeing it all again. "So he pegged his old man," I said. "That's bold, Cathy." I looked to the ridge and imagined that drunk man's eyes when he got hit.

"Sam's like that I guess. Does exactly what he shouldn't do at just the right moment," she said and laughed.

"I got a piece of it. I remember."

She got quiet a minute and looked at the shack. I felt her drift even though she sat right next to me.

"So what did the old man do?" I finished the sandwich, slapped my hands on my pants.

"Well, he looked at us in this way that was different than before, when he thought we couldn't see him. He wore a white T-shirt with sweat stains in the folds of his belly and under his arms. It was real hot. I froze when I saw his eyes. They were full of rage. You know rage in the eyes? Like that. I can't describe it. I wanted to run; I was so scared, but I couldn't. My body went rigid.

"He came flying down that hill. Sounded like a wild pig smashing through the brush. I almost peed in my pants."

She pointed to where the tunnel opened, where the old man must have burst through. It wasn't too far from where we sat, and I imagined how long it would take to cover the distance.

"But Sam was ready. I remember his back was to me, and I saw his hand pulling that wrench out of his back pocket and hiding it. Then they were a knot, fighting in the dirt. I couldn't see who was winning, and I couldn't move. But just a few minutes later, a few seconds maybe, my father stood up and Sam didn't."

"The wrench?"

"I don't know. I guess Sam still had it. Yeah, he had it. Just shut up and listen till I finish. Well, it was my turn you know. He'd hit me before, but never crazy. He was harder like that on Sam. But I could see this was going to be different. I curled up, hid my face. I don't know. I still remember his voice, this deep, dusty drawl telling me to get up and come over there."

"Did you do it?" I asked.

"No. What happened is Sam got up, tackled him. He was a mess, blood all over his face and his arms."

"Damn." I let a second or two slip by quietly. "You didn't really know why you were coming here, did you, Cath?"

"No, I didn't really. I'd just been thinking. That's all. I'm not in an easy spot you know." She looked at me with a question in her eyes.

I shrugged. "I can see that," I said.

"I'm surprised you've let it go this long. Do you want a drink?"

She did so we walked back to the shack, and opened the basket.

"It's kind of spooky being in here, now that I remember what happened," she said. A chill went through my spine. I looked around the shack for evidence that the ghosts were really gone. Maybe they weren't. I poured the pineapple juice into two cups, gave one to Cathy, then lifted mine as if toasting. We drank the cold juice. It went well with the sandwiches.

"How'd you get away from the dogs today?"

"Well, I didn't tell him I wasn't coming. I'll have to go back later and feed them."

"Sam won't take care of it?"

"Probably not." Her eyes looked down and were lost in the shade from the bill of her cap.

"Cath, how do you really feel about all this?" I took her cup and set it on top of the egg crate.

"Are we talking about crimes now?" She shifted, tucked her leg underneath her and wrapped her arms around her stomach.

"There aren't any real crimes in the dog business. People are just too busy, I guess. At least that's the way it seems to me."

She looked up. Her dark eyes trying to reach something inside me. I could feel it, her desire for my strength. "Legget, will you tell me what you think about the greyhounds?"

I hesitated. Cathy added, "I mean, you know what goes on. You know how they're treated. Or do you? Tell me what you know and what you think about it. I really need to know."

"OK, I know that most of them don't become racers. The ones that do last two maybe three years and then they're killed. Some trainers put a bullet through their heads, some dogs get electrocuted or starved, some are dumped in a place like this. I know some get their ears cut off so they can't be traced. I don't know which is worst. No, I know. The whole thing is sick. It makes me sick. But, I'll tell you the truth, Cath. It happens all over the fucking country, and no one can stop it."

Cathy nodded and stared.

"I've heard that some trainers use rabbits to tease up the dogs. Live lure. I've heard they'll stick a rabbit on the end of a pole and get the hounds to chase. The trainer will let the hounds catch the rabbit, chew on it a while then yank it away, and on with the chase again until the rabbit dies. Hell, I've even heard that some trainers use cats and puppies. They'll get them out of the classifieds in the newspaper. And that chokes me up. No, I couldn't let that happen, but I do. See what I mean? I can't follow these jerks everywhere. I can't arrest. All I can do, as an Animal Control officer, is fill out some forms. And that doesn't do a whole lot of good. Cath, I lost my job because of your boss, Dr. Fielding. I used to think he was a great man. What kills me is that somehow I know he is great. Can you be great and evil at the same time? I don't know. I'd like my fucking job back. I don't have much more."

Cathy looked surprised. She waved her hands.

"Wait, Legget. How did you lose your job?"

"It's a long story."

"You need to tell me." She put her hand on my shoulder.

"I don't know about that. It's your turn. Don't take this hard, but it seems you're sleeping with the wrong side now. You can imagine I'm wondering about it."

She started to pack our things into the basket. Then she sat still and stared out into nothing. She was thinking. There were so many things to think about, I couldn't guess what. "Come on, Cath."

"Wait." She stood up, moved to the door and blocked my exit. "I'll help you, and you'll get your job back. What do you say?"

"It's not that easy." I wasn't convinced she meant it.

A tightening in her lip told me she was serious, and that she wouldn't let it go as quick as all that. "When Sam tackled my father, you know, after he'd already lost the fight, he didn't have much left, bleeding, knowing he was going to get hurt, and he did, Legget. My dad got that monkey wrench and laid it across his forehead. The tiniest red crack you could imagine sprouted over his skin. God, I can still see it." She put her forehead in her hand and rubbed it like the crack was on her. "It stopped him. Sam looked dead. Made Dad sober in a flash. Sam didn't die of course, but he can't remember things anymore. He forgets what day it is or how to get home or how to use a telephone. Different things. And you understand now, he took that crack for me. He's my brother!"

I had no brothers or sisters, but I understood. I just watched her, letting the quiet fill up the shack.

"OK, I don't like what they do on the farm, Legget. No, I hate it. OK? I want it to stop. But I can't do it. I can't betray my brother. And Dr. Fielding, Jesus, I don't know what he'd do." Her voice trailed off and she caved in with her arms wrapping around her stomach, and I stood up and tried to pull her close, but she backed away

"I really didn't know why I wanted to come here. But I do now. I can't do this anymore. I can't do it to Sam. We've got to stop right here. I'm sorry. I can't see you anymore."

I swallowed and it felt like she'd dropped a stone into my stomach. I opened my mouth but nothing came out. Then I caught hold and steeled up.

"Well," I said. "I can't promise you I'll stay away," I said it because I thought I was supposed to, but I felt that stone and nothing else.

She looked at me and I could see all the straight lines in her face, nothing soft anymore. She had that look a woman gives you when she means something is gone with no way back. "It's done," she said and lifted the basket and walked out.

Chapter 11

The first time I was assigned a route I found a .22 in the glove box of the truck and a dirty-blue bottle of antacid. At first, I'd thought the pistol was a BB gun because it looked like a toy you'd buy at the K-Mart, but it was heavy, and when I started to fiddle with it, I found the bullets and knew it was a .22. I'd guessed it had been left by the ACO before me, who'd retired to a double-wide near Myakka State Park with a bunch of dogs. It reminded me of my own dreams of having dogs and land like that. That's where I wanted to end up. But people said he was crazy, cared more about dogs than people. I could almost see why. It couldn't hurt to have a pistol on the job, and the small caliber led me to believe it was for shooting raccoons or rats that showed signs of rabies.

After I'd cleaned out the truck, I'd put it in my bag, then hid it under the bed when I got home. I hadn't thought then that I'd ever be pulling it out, but now things were happening around me that I didn't think would ever happen.

I couldn't sleep. I sat on the couch with Cal and nursed a little glass of Dewars, but it didn't taste right. The television spit out noise and static like a drunk old woman. I never found comfort in it anyway, and I didn't think I could sleep till I'd seen what had to be seen. I needed to know why Cathy was scared of the farm. I was the only one; I was the one who had to go in first. And I had little to lose. It wasn't even a question of losing anything. It was a question of seeing with my own eyes the reason for all this.

I found a pair of pants that were loose around the ankles and dark, a pair of tennis shoes and a dark shirt. I took the .22 and separated the parts on the kitchen table. I cleaned the pieces while the radio played. It was dirty, but I wasn't worried about it shooting. I would be lucky if it didn't shoot. But I knew I had to take it with me. I wasn't losing another fight.

In the back closet was an Army flashlight I had acquired from somewhere. I tore through my junk till I found it on the bottom of a box filled with paperwork. The flashlight had a curved head, so you could hook it on your shirt and the beam would shine straight ahead. It had a red filter on the front, which made the light red and less detectable at night. It needed batteries. I laced my shoes, turned on the porch light, and locked the trailer.

I had trouble finding a place for the pistol. It bounced around in my front pocket; in the back, it felt like it would fall out, and in the belt I had the same problem. So I just dropped it on the seat and decided to worry about it when I got there.

First I drove to the 7-Eleven at the corner and bought a pack of batteries and cigars for six dollars. It took me twenty minutes to drive to the entrance of Diamond Kennel. I sat in the truck at the top of the dirt road, next to the white fence, and smoked. There were a couple of lights on in the buildings, but I didn't see shadows, and it didn't seem like there was anyone there. I didn't know if Sam lived there or not.

I parked the truck a ways up past the entrance to Diamond on the hump of a ditch, beneath the branches of an oak tree. My cigar tasted good, and I felt strange sitting under the tree. The gun was on the seat, and I thought about it a minute. Then imagined what I would do if Sam showed up all of a sudden. I wondered what I would do if I found the farm. All I really wanted was to see it. I didn't want to shoot anyone, but I wouldn't lose another fight.

My truck was fifty feet from the dirt road. I walked the distance, then turned around. Since there weren't any streetlights, the truck was invisible. I made a note of how the branches over the truck looked like a hand, so if I needed to get back in a hurry, I'd have a good chance of finding it fast. My keys jangled in my pocket, so I took some bills out of my wallet and wadded up the keys in the money, then stuffed them back in.

There was a patch of field behind the white fence that had a few palm trees. The moon was bright against the knee-high grass. There might be water out there. There might be rattle snakes. I tested the flashlight for the fifth time. From the edge of the field behind the fence, it lit up about ten feet, like a red tunnel ahead of me.

Before I walked down the field, I let my shoulders down, trying to shake out the stiffness. I cracked my neck and breathed deep. There were cars driving by on the highway. I could hear them and see the headlights stutter in the trees. For a minute I heard music and crouched down low, but it wasn't near enough. I was able to hear sounds I had never listened to before: wind, leaves. I kneeled down, looked ahead at Diamond Kennels, and listened to the barking of a greyhound. They didn't bark all that much, so I was worried. But I didn't see any people.

I tried to imagine what Sam would look like walking through the cages. It made me see things that weren't there.

My footsteps seemed loud in the grass. Walking across the field took forever; the whole time those buildings got bigger, and real. Chain link fencing, and then quick, dark movements of the dogs at night. They could feel me coming closer. It wasn't good; it was like an alarm. I must have found every wet puddle of mud out there. And when I finally crouched near the dirt of the little parking lot across from the kennel, my pants and shoes were soaked. I was sweating, breathing hard. But my eyes were sharp as an animal's.

The greyhounds perked up. I could see their eyes as shiny as water. There were two close to me, stiff and dark. A light was on in the back of the building where I had first met Cathy, but I saw no others. There was no movement in the building, and the door was closed with a lock and chain. One last deep breath and I was standing, walking across the little parking lot past the greyhound truck. I nudged close to it when I walked by, then stayed close to the building. A couple of greyhounds watched me sneak around the cages. One growled, and I stopped. I shined the flashlight in his eyes. He stopped growling and moved to the back of the cage.

Walking next to the side of the building where Sam's office was, I looked for a window. There were no lights on in the office. I looked through the window and saw nothing, and I wasn't going to shine the light inside. I listened but there was no sound, so I sat down on the cement slab in front of the door.

There was nothing here for me to find, nothing to see that I hadn't already seen. I could break in and hope to find the steroids, but that would prove nothing. Fielding could come up with a prescription. John wouldn't approve. If I was here to get my job back, then I needed to find something that would make everybody forget how I found it. It had to be that big. I knew it was there.

I started walking around the building, looking through trees for a path with treads and wear that might lead me to the farm. I ended up where Cal had been kicked. Clusters of aloe plants stuck out like little spears under the red beam of the flashlight. Bugs stuck to the sweat on my face. As I wiped them away, I saw the cut in the trees. The husk of a palm tree lay across the dirt path like a speed bump.

The sand was fine on the trail, and my shoes sunk in. I was breathing hard, anxious, ready to see it all before me. I pulled my shirt off and wiped sweat from my face. It was a long trail, and I didn't know what was at the other end or what I would run into, so I turned off the flashlight and walked slower. There was plenty of room; two men could have walked the trail side by side. I felt like a hunter. I felt like it all came down to this.

The trees cut away suddenly, and the shadows disappeared. The bulk of space in front of me seemed huge, but it was dark. There were other shapes, one that looked like a truck, and movement, little darts of light and dark under the building. I walked forward slowly, hesitating with each step like I was in a minefield. The ground started to rise slightly. My steps were shorter in the dirt and the dirt was softer than before. I made it to the top of this little hill and looked around. The shape of a roof reflected in the moonlight, bright like steel or aluminum. I heard only the wind and my breath. I could barely catch my breathing. The smell. There was a sick smell, sweet and raw like death. I aimed the flashlight straight ahead and flicked it on. A spot of red light on the flank of the building. Wire cages just below a tin roof. The shuffle of dogs on cement. The smell.

They exploded. Like a bomb, their barks and yelps burst into the quiet. I ducked and scanned with the flashlight over a small bulldozer, over the building. The dogs barked and barked. I didn't know what to do but run down the small hill to hide. The truck was too far, no trees, the only way out was back. I leaned on my knees, took two steps, turned off the flashlight. Maybe no one was there. Maybe I was the only man for miles.

I heard a door slam, then, "Marion! Quién es?!"

I was imagining it. It was Mexican. "Quién es?!" Again.

Who's there? it said. Jesus, who's there. I scurried down the hill, but my shoe caught on something hard beneath me, and I fell. Not headlong, but my knee buckled and I dipped low, put my hands in front to catch myself, and I hit something. The ground was covered with shapes, rocks or piles of dirt, old rope. My hands knew the shapes beneath them but I couldn't make the connection. I couldn't catch on, and pulled my legs together. The voice was coming closer. My hands were wet, something wet. "Quién es, la puta?!"

Then I realized the shapes were dogs. I was in a hole filled with dead hounds. The rope had tied them together.

I dropped the flashlight. The voice came closer. I stood and ran. I heard my heart and my breaths and my legs, then suddenly another explosion, and to my right a thousand pebbles slapping through the trees and brush. He was shooting. The Mexican was shooting and coming at me. I thought I could feel him behind me, but I wouldn't look. I couldn't think, and I couldn't see where I was running. I knew the trail by the dirt, and my arms smacked trees and bark and leaves. I hadn't run that far and that hard in years. When I couldn't run anymore, I fell to the side in the bushes.

I lay there panting, imagining how far I was from my truck. It had to be far because I hadn't even reached the main kennel. My gums burned, every breath deeper and slower in the bushes. The Mexican did not appear. I had expected him to be right behind me. He wouldn't shoot me on the ground.

Finally, I caught my breath. I lay still for a minute, listening. I heard nothing, so, I pulled myself out of the bushes and wiped off the dirt caked around the back of my neck. Where was the Mexican? I checked for my keys, and they were still in the pocket. The flashlight was gone, but I was used to the dark, and I would never turn that thing on again.

The bushes made a lot of noise. My head was foamed up, cluttered. Suddenly I remembered the hole I had fallen into. The greyhounds in the hole. That's how they got rid of them. Tied them together so they couldn't get out, so they could pull them in. It was easier to breed more. Keep breeding and breeding. I turned up the path and bumped right into him. He had been standing there in the dark the whole time, waiting. The last thing I saw was the golden butt of the shotgun flashing between his hip and my cheek.

* * *

I woke to the sound of engines. They seemed close, and the sound vibrated against my face. Something thick had caked in my mouth. It was warm, and I felt heavy. The sound of the engine continued to fade in and out as if closer, then farther. The bulldozer plowed to the top of the dirt mound, then pushed the dirt over the hole. I watched the bulldozer through the links of the fence. A dog was standing next to me panting. Its tongue flicked up and down.

I leaned on my elbow, my head propped just inches from the cement floor. My legs were moist. It smelled like piss and dog sweat. There were two dogs in the cage with me. They seemed huge above me. I was afraid to move too much because my body was sore, but it didn't seem damaged. The Mexican was in the bulldozer covering the hole filled with dead greyhounds. The smoke from his cigarette mingled with smoke from the small pipe of the machine. They bred as many dogs as they could, then culled the ones who couldn't run. They were dead, lost money to feeding and space.

It must have been late afternoon because the air was cooler and the clouds seemed very close. The sun had set mostly. There was still light, an orange smear behind the gray clouds above me. I tried to stand but bumped my head against the top of the cage. I sat with my back bent and my palms against the wet cement. My left hand was in chrome-yellow piss. The dogs were at the front of the cage. They paced when I moved. They were nervous.

"Hey!" The bulldozer was too loud. My throat was sore and dry.

I looked around the cage. There was a tin bucket toward the front filled with water. I crawled to it, but there were gnats and roaches floating on the top. Cages and dogs were on both sides of me. My cage was in the middle of twenty or so. There was a dog in every one. Puppies mostly. Breeding farm. I knew they would let me out of the cage. They had to let me out. They probably had just waited for me to wake. I was awake.

"Hey, Fuck!" The bulldozer pushed dirt over the bodies of the greyhounds.

One dog was brindle, the other light brown or fawn. The brindle looked familiar as it paced near the water, then dropped its head to slop at the bowl. Its head came up and a roach clung to his lower lip.

"Hey, hey!" The bulldozer had just covered the hole and was smoothing out the dirt. The Mexican looked over his shoulder once, but didn't acknowledge me.

"Come here, boy." I pushed the two dogs to the far end of the cage then crawled to the front under the shade. I pushed the water bucket out of the way and inspected the cage door. It was locked with a four-inch Master Lock. The other cages just had metal pins through the handles.

I looked into the alley under the roof of the building for people, but saw no one. The bulldozer cut off as I was pressed against the cage front. I spun around and skinned my knees badly as I moved to the other side of the cage. The greyhounds skittered to the other end. He was climbing down from the seat of the bulldozer.

"Hey, replica!"

"Fuck you, gringo," he said lightly. I didn't believe he had spoken at first.

"Let me out of this cage." The dogs started to sniff at me. One came forward and licked my face.

"I can't do that, gringo." He checked something on the bulldozer's engine, then prepared to climb back up.

"I'm not a gringo." I pushed the dog away. It yelped as if I had injured it.

The Mexican turned quickly. "Sleep tight, gringo." He turned on the bulldozer and drove around the corner of the building, then shut it off. I waited, pressed against the wire, for him to return. I could not remember any Spanish.

The smell of piss was strong. I was alert. The dogs watched everything. When the two dogs lunged to the front of the cage, knocking over the water bucket, I knew someone was coming down the alley. I pushed between the two dogs and watched also. A pair of legs, visible up to the knee, came up the hallway. They were men's legs; it wasn't the Mexican.

When the legs were right in front of the cage, I yelled. He was startled. He stopped, then came closer. "Hey, is that you Legget? Boy, how'd you get in there?"

"Let me out of this, Sam." I reached through a gap in the cage for Sam's neck.

"No way. You'll try to kill us. I'll have to wait till you calm down and see things clearly."

"I see clearly right now, Sam. You can't leave me in this fucking cage."

"See? You said 'fucking'. That proves you're still angry. I can't let you out."

The Mexican came up the alley. He pushed a wheelbarrow.

"Qué pasó?" Sam walked toward him, pushed the wheelbarrow down and walked the Mexican outside. I scrambled to the other side of the cage. They were at the edge of the building. Sam's back was to me, but his arms were raised, pointing back, as if he were giving instructions. The Mexican nodded many times.

The Mexican did not return to the alley. None of the dogs were fed or watered, though they barked and cried for an hour. I didn't know if it was because of me or if it was the usual practice. I sat Indian style at the back of the cage so I could see the sky.

I didn't think they would kill me like they killed the greyhounds. They wouldn't kill a man. It was not the same thing to them. It couldn't be. Dr. Fielding wouldn't allow this to happen, and it was his farm. But then I had all the evidence I needed. If I got out, I would return.

After it was dark a while, the flood lights popped on. I must have dozed off because when I opened my eyes, there were Sam and Dr. Fielding standing together in the dusted light. They marched over the graveyard, and then to the cages.

My first impulse was to yell, but I didn't. I wasn't crazy yet. Fielding's hair flew back in the wind. He stared at the ground while taking long steps. Sam had to jog to keep up with him. Fielding whipped past the cages without looking at me, but Sam glanced quickly. The door to the alley opened. I listened. I heard Fielding's voice and a door or maybe the wheelbarrow again, then one set of footsteps coming up the alley of the cages.

It was Sam, and he was carrying the shotgun with the barrel pointed to the ground.

"Where's Dr. Fielding?" I asked and moved to the back of the cage. I couldn't stretch my legs out.

Sam's black eyes were hard as he split open the barrel over his forearm, then pulled two red shells from his pocket.

"Watch this, motherfucker," Sam said and shoved the shells into the slots and cracked the barrel back together.

I swallowed, and my head started racing with crazy thoughts, and I grabbed the cage wires and shook and watched the barrel of the shotgun slip through the cage and stare at me like a dark eye.

"They'll catch you, Sam. They'll start looking for me."

"Fuck you."

I lunged forward and tried to grab the barrel of the gun, but there wasn't enough cold metal to hold on to, and it slipped through my fingers as Sam laughed and pulled the barrel back and pumped it.

He backed up and aimed so the barrel wasn't anywhere near the cage door, and I felt my body shiver and warm piss filling my crotch, and I thought of nothing but my dog alone in the trailer and who would come to get him.

Then I heard steps again and Fielding's voice erupt in the quiet of my head.

"Hey! Sam! What did I tell you!" Fielding yelled. I opened my eyes and saw him jogging toward us.

Sam turned to look once at Fielding, then turned back to me and rested his cheek against the stock. I watched his finger move over the trigger like slow motion and started shaking my head, no, but it was coming. I could almost feel the thrust of the shells like a shove against my chest.

"Hey!"

I heard Fielding yell again, a second before the explosion and sparks of fire from the barrel, then the ringing in my ear and the splatter around me. Moist, running fluid on my face. Flesh caught up in my lips, up my nose, and the terrible ringing in my head. Fielding grabbed the shotgun, ripped it from Sam's grip, and held it at his side.

"Open it," he shouted, spit flying from his lips.

"Pedro's got the key." Sam looked puzzled.

"Jesus Christ, get the goddamn key," Fielding shouted.

Then I realized I wasn't dead. I looked at my hands and they were covered with black skin and fur and blood and flesh of every color. I let my breath out and and looked at the cage floor, and one of the greyhounds that had been there was on the cement without a head. I felt the bile and vomit rise in my throat and couldn't take my eyes off the headless carcass and the oozing shit from where its head was. I started to moan and I was crazy, someone else, had to get away from these people, these fucking killers.

"Let's go, Legget." I turned around. The Mexican was there with a baseball bat. "He ain't going to use it unless I tell him, Legget. Come on." Sam had a blue towel in his hand.

I stepped down and out of the cage, stumbled, then found my balance and took the towel from Sam. I was too tired to fight. I just wanted to get out, to prepare. Dr. Fielding stood by the open door of the alley. He had a hand in a pocket, and he swayed back and forth slowly. I used the towel, but it was foolish. It just rubbed the shit and blood into my skin.

"Where's my shirt you sick motherfucker?" I dropped the towel at Sam's feet.

"Did you come with a shirt?" Sam's face was bright. He smiled, a laugh just behind his lips.

"I came with a shirt." I turned toward the door. I couldn't look at the crazy fuck.

Dr. Fielding looked down. His face was flushed pink. Moving out of the doorway as I passed, he said, "Give him your fucking shirt, Sam."

His voice was loud and forced. He looked at me while Sam pulled off his shirt. "Just remember I let you out, Legget."

"I won't forget anything." I pulled the shirt over my head.

"Nobody gives a shit about the dogs, Legget. That's the only reason you're still alive," Dr. Fielding said.

"I don't know what you're talking about."

"I know you don't."

"You think this is over? You're crazy."

Fielding grabbed my shoulder and looked down into my eyes like a killer.

"Listen to me close. Think about it. I let you walk away. Maybe you're still good for something, dog catcher. You hear me? Last chance." He shoved me toward the open field.

I walked away. Dr. Fielding's voice rose from behind. "You can't hurt me, Legget!"

As I walked back to my truck, I heard the Mexican yelling and then Fielding's voice and theirs floated to me and landed at my back like knife cuts. I couldn't believe I was alive. And somewhere in my head I remembered when I was a boy and had snuck out of the house after my mother had fallen asleep. I had stood in her doorway and listened for her breaths in rhythm, then walked out to where the men gathered.

They had stacked wooden crates in a circle. I had snuck through the darkness, across grass and dirt to where they huddled, twenty, thirty, maybe more. They smoked reefer-like cigarettes and long, hand-rolled cigars.

They were loud, bare-chested, dark. Sweat gathered in the creases of their close bodies as they argued and held wads of money in the air. They had pit bulls in the crates outside the circle. I hid behind the stacked strawberry crates, shivered and peeked through the slats. They didn't notice me. I was a small boy who did not understand their language.

I watched two Mexicans bring their crates into the middle of the circle. Floodlights were on in the shacks behind them. A bonfire roared outside the circle where others drank beer and argued. One Mexican was young, a boy with long hair like a woman's. The other, a fat man with powerful shoulders, and a booming voice. The fat man taunted the young boy with shouts, spit flying from his mouth, sticking to his black moustache. He held a large branch covered with leaves in his left hand and bent over near the dog's crate. The young boy squatted, talking to his dog in the crate, then rose tall and thin near the fat man.

They released the dogs together, then stepped back. The fat man shook the branch behind his white pit bull. The dogs paced around each other like fancy horses. The boy's pit bull was smaller and black but faster. It was the first to lunge. The boy yelled, and I ducked behind the crates as the black dog went for the throat of the other.

When the dogs struck, I saw a dark knot rolling and jerking between the two men. Dust formed close to the ground. One dog whimpered, it's cry rising above all the shouts of the men. Then I saw blood. A red stream shot into the sky and landed thickly in the dust. The dogs unknotted. The boy rushed forward to his black dog, but the old man yelled and the boy moved away.

The white pit bull had the neck of the other in its jaw. The white bull shook it and dragged it along the dirt. I saw blood and pink flesh. The white bull trotted with the limp body in its mouth. The fat man grabbed the back legs of his dog, while laughing. He flipped the white bull on its side and it let go of the other dog.

The boy rushed forward to his still pit bull, and kicked it fiercely with his pointed boot. I saw the point of the dark boot strike the face and eye of the dead dog. I ran home as the boot struck the dead pit bull again in my head and the boy's curses rang in the air like the ringing in my ears just then when I saw my truck under the tree branches shaped like a hand.

I was coming back. Fielding was crazy to let me go. I was coming back, and not alone next time. I started the truck and reached over for a Sweet, then jabbed the truck lighter in and took a deep breath. Goddamn if I wasn't coming back. But I needed some help, someone who could make an arrest for the dead greyhounds, maybe kidnapping, and put things back on track.

Chapter 12

Chip Dario lived at the end of a nameless road over a small metal bridge, on a swamp that trailed its way to the Kasahatchee River. His townhouse was one of only three in that area built in the seventies. The developer had gone out of business and left the three buildings to themselves. But since Dario and his wife, and son, had already purchased the house, they lived there now, and, with their son, were the only ones in the building.

The land he lived on had been declared an environmentally protected zone, part of the bird sanctuary amendment of the early eighties that allowed certain wild sections of the county to be protected from builders. Of course, their townhouses had been built long before that. And the builders had gone out of business before the bird sanctuary had been declared. What it meant to Dario was simple. He owned a piece of the land that no one else could ever build on.

I had no idea if Dario would be home, but it was an easy chance to take on a Sunday. I hoped he was in one of those weekend moods that took him out into the garage or the boathouse around the saw grass, the cattails, the alligator nest, the great blue herons, and his boats. If so, my arrival would suit the day well, and he would talk.

I remembered the little metal and cement bridge with the broken pylon in front of his private road and flipped the Luv into a low gear while turning. Cal enjoyed the ride. He stuck his head out the window and let his tongue flap. He yawned and squinted, then gulped the air.

The townhouses were two stories, with high, steeply pitched roofs. The walls outside were cabin brown. There was a black Bronco in the yard next to a litter of toys: a tricycle, a wagon, beach balls, and a plastic motorcycle. I saw Dario bent inside the hood of the Bronco. His stomach was pressed flat against the fender well, and it puffed out on the sides. He stood up with a ratchet in his hand when he heard my truck. His hair was stiff and unkempt as if he hadn't combed it all day, and there was a streak of grease on his white chest. His son came out of the open garage. He had dark hair like Dario's, but with bright, steady eyes.

I let Cal out the side and waved.

"He won't bite," I yelled when Dario's son went up to play with Cal. I knew they would take to each other right away.

Dario tossed the ratchet into a tool chest and sighed. "Now I'm going to have to get him a dog," he said as the boy and Cal ran toward the side of the house where I could see the water.

I shook hands with Dario, then put mine in my pockets.

"How ya' doing, Legget?" He wiped his hands on his shorts.

"I'm all right. Well, not so good, really. Sorry to barge in on you like this, but ..."

Dario looked at me hard, then dropped the prop bar and lowered the hood to his Bronco. He spit once on the engine before he closed it, then clapped his hands together. The hood slammed down, and Dario looked at me again, studying my eyes. I was standing by the driver's side mirror. I shrugged and waited.

He leaned against the front of the truck. "Boy seems to like your dog."

"He doesn't even know the dog's name, and he's off playing. Hell, he probably won't want to come back with me." I stepped closer and wiped sweat off my forehead.

Dario turned to watch his wife come out of the garage door. She was a regular-looking woman, a little chubby, dark hair pulled back into a workday ponytail. She wore sandals, red shorts, and a white shirt with a V-neck. She had a good tan, and a pleasant smile. Coming out of the shelter of the garage, she put her hand over her eyes to block the sun and get a good look at me. She came up behind Dario, but didn't touch him.

"Hey, Chip. I saw Marcus with that dog and wondered. Hello," she said to me.

Dario introduced us, though we had met before. It was awkward. LuAnn invited me in for tea or a beer, and I followed Dario through the garage and into the kitchen, where I sat at a small breakfast table with a glass top and place mats, and a bowl of wooden fruit.

Dario washed his hands in the kitchen sink, then went out the garage door again. I heard him calling his son, Marcus, from the garage. In the kitchen, LuAnn poured a beer into a glass for me, and then tea for herself and Dario.

"What are you doing down here today?" She set the beer down on the glass table.

I hoped Dario would come back in before I had to answer. It would have taken too much explaining, and I wasn't sure she even remembered who I was. I doubted Dario told her much about his job.

"I work for Animal Control."

"Oh?" She sat at the table, and crossed her legs. She had bad spider veins in her upper thigh. I looked away.

"I've worked with your husband quite a few times. We patrol the same area." I sipped through the foam on my beer.

"He doesn't talk much about work really but I recognize you from someplace." Her voice was sweet and honest. Someone you could trust. She looked older from close up. No makeup, but sharp lines around her lips, and a brown birthmark, just a dot, under her nose.

"I've been here before," I said, a little embarrassed.

She blushed. "So that's it. It must have been the boat. Chip took you out on the boat, right?"

"He did." I smiled, and she laughed a little.

Dario came back into the kitchen with Marcus under the palm of his hand. They made a lot of noise, and shuffled past the chairs.

"Where's Cal?"

Marcus turned and pointed to the garage. "He's sitting in the garage!" His voice was loud and scratchy.

I started to get up, but Dario put out his hand. "I'll bring him some water."

"I'm not so sure he'll stay where he is, Dario." I followed him outside, then watched Cal wag his tail, and drink water from a stainless steel bowl. Dario stood above the dog, too, and there was another awkward silence. Dario's garage was filled with tools, sports equipment, car parts, boxes stuffed with things.

"How's your boat running?"

"Good. I was going to take it out today, tour the swamp, maybe hit the river, do a little fishing."

"Yeah? Good day for it." I reached down to Cal and petted him. He smelled like swamp gas, but there was light in his wet eyes. He had had fun playing with the boy.

Dario relaxed. I could see his shoulders give up their stiffness. "Yeah. The whole swamp is off limits, and then about half a mile up the river. After that, there's houses. It's like a little world over here. No other boats, no fishing or hunting, and a cop living on the edge of it. It's just perfect. And best of all, I retire in eleven years."

I thought eleven years was a hell of a long time. Cal got anxious, wanted to go back out by the swamp. I was worried about alligators, but Dario let his kid run around out there, so it must be OK.

"Let me show you what I've done since the last time." Dario motioned me to follow him out of the garage, then around the side of the house.

"Ever get any neighbors?" There was one complete house next to Dario's, under the same roof.

"I don't think they can sell it. Hell, I'd like to move my things in there."

His back yard was perfect. The grass was lush and well cared for. They had edged around the little porch and weeded in the garden boxes that hedged the back of the house. There was an above-ground pool on the far side of the lawn, about four feet high with a red cedar deck built around its back side. A lot of toys for a cop.

The boat was a fourteen-foot swamp swimmer. The engine and the fan weighed down the back. It was pulled three-quarters of the way out of the water. Dario walked over to it and straightened the hull, but it flopped right back over to the side. The captain's chair was high up in the back. I remembered Dario in that seat with the wind blowing his cheeks and hair.

Dario walked around it once, seemingly forgetting I was there. He was full of his life here, at his townhouse, on his swamp. The other world, the one with Animal Control officers and crimes and revenge, seemed far away. I didn't know if I had the courage or the cruelty, whatever it took, to drag him into my problem. He wasn't even a friend, really. The last time I had been at his house, it was different.

He had been considering a dog, and since he knew me from patrol, he had asked about some animals at the pound. We had talked a little about shepherds and their fur, huskies, pit bulls, retrievers. He had been partial to a golden retriever, and we had had one at Animal Control. Dario invited me to dinner and I brought the dog. Marcus had been at his grandmother's, and we had the dinner, talked some more. I had done it as a favor, and there was a free meal involved, the boat ride.

They'd decided not to take the dog, and I didn't pressure them. I didn't want to come back and have to haul him away. But, I thought, there is that between us. If there was such a thing as karma, I wondered if you had to take it.

"Let's do it!" I shouted as Dario climbed into the air boat.

He didn't need much convincing. He turned the key, and the engine choked, the fan spun over, and the hull lifted slightly off the grass, as if it were a small dragon coming to life.

The boy charged out the back door, and Cal bolted from the rose bushes where he had been exploring. I called the dog over, and he came, but with hesitation. He sat by my leg, and we watched Marcus beg his father to take him with us.

LuAnn appeared from inside the house and stood on the back porch with her arms crossed. She didn't look angry or even defiant, but Dario saw her and suddenly the engine was off.

Cal was relieved.

"What's the matter?"

Dario looked at the ground and mumbled something about the choke or the exhaust.

"We're taking the Bayliner." He walked behind the tool shed.

It looked like Marcus was coming, so I figured Cal would come too. LuAnn came back out of the house as Cal and I followed everybody around the tree. She had a blue thermos, and a baseball cap for each of her boys.

"Would you like a hat, Legget?"

The Bayliner was the same size as the air boat, but it had a regular outboard engine. Marcus called it a Black Max. He was excited, and knew the boat routine well. He found three life jackets under the paneling, put one on, and handed me the other. The third one, he placed next to the driver's seat where his father would sit.

I had to pick Cal up to get him in the boat. Marcus helped me with the back legs, and we got him in. I had Marcus hold him while Dario started the boat. He let it idle for a minute, and went over to kiss his wife and take the thermos. Marcus petted Cal, and I found a seat near Dario's. It was hot, and there were mosquitoes whipping around my face.

The far side of the swamp was wild with weeds and logs and trees, and a thick skin of brown algae near the bank. I noticed lots of mud, and sandpipers in the mud and fiddler crabs in the holes all over the mud. The water spread into a canal that curved west around the other two townhouses.

Dario steered the little boat into the canal, made a wide turn around a corner, then went straight for the middle. It was cooler when the boat started gliding up the middle of the canal. Dario stood up while he steered, and Marcus sat at the front of the boat looking down into the water.

"I think of that old Bogart movie, *The African Queen*, when I ride down this canal. They used to talk about building a nuclear power plant a ways down, can you believe that?" He looked back quickly to check our course.

I leaned closer so he could hear me over the gurgling sounds of the engine. "It's always amazed me what people will do for money."

I thought of the body tour, as if it were someone else that had done it, and I had only just heard of it.

"Look what you did just for a boat ride, unless you're after my wife." Marcus looked at his father strangely. "In fact, Legget, you can't begin to imagine what I've seen people do for money."

I pushed Cal to his chest while Dario turned the boat along a curve in the canal. The trees were denser, and looped over the top of the canal like a tunnel. Dario slowed the boat, then turned it off. Maybe he was telling me something.

"This is the best spot on the whole canal. Manatees come here." He pointed to the water.

Marcus swirled his arm over the edge, and I noticed Dario watching him closely out of the corner of his eye. I let Cal stand, then walk to the bow. Marcus petted the dog, then looked back over the edge. He was a quiet kid.

LuAnn had packed iced tea in the blue thermos. Dario passed the thermos around after taking a long swig. Marcus tipped the thermos up with both hands, while Cal licked the tea that trickled down. Dario let the boat float toward the bank. He had lifted the engine with a heavy grunt, then locked it. Marcus checked the paddles.

"Have you ever been to the race track?" I looked over the edge and saw the bottom of the canal. The water was pretty clear, but brownish still, and the bottom was muck. Shiners darted in and out of the algae.

"Not really." Dario took his seat again behind the wheel.

"You understand the track, the greyhounds?" It was more a statement than a question. I leaned up and watched Dario's eyes, but the sun was bright. The boat swirled, and I was under the shade of overhanging trees, then back in the sun. I started to feel dizzy.

"Why'd you come here, Legget?" He motioned to Marcus, who climbed around Cal and sat on his father's lap. "I told you as much as I can about Holton. It's not that important."

"It is if your fucking job's at stake. Sorry." Marcus looked up brightly.

"I don't think anyone even read that report. It will all blow over soon enough. You know how crazy it is." Marcus wanted to get down and swim. Dario stripped the boy to his underwear and tightened the life jacket. He dunked his son over the edge of the boat that was in deep water. Cal barked at him when he dropped the boy. The boat whirled around, and almost smacked the boy on the head. Dario used the paddle to stop it. "Sometimes it's better just to let things be, Legget," Dario said.

"Do you know Dr. Fielding?" I took the paddle, and tucked it back under the rim.

He nodded and watched his boy thrash in the water. It wasn't that deep. The life jacket held him up by his ears. Cal continued to bark and put his paws on the edge of the boat to look over at Marcus.

"Sure. Doesn't he own that hospital downtown?"

"Dexter's Field." The boat settled against the mud on the shore.

"Will you let me tell you a story?" I said. Cal gave up on Marcus, came back to me, and put his head on my leg. I scooped some water from over the edge into the empty thermos and poured it out for Cal. Dario pulled Marcus from the water like a soaked rat, set him down and toweled him off.

"I've got nothing else to do right now," he said.

I told him about Fielding's bribe that I had accepted, what I had seen at the farm, and finally how Fielding had got me fired, then what had happened last night. Dario wasn't surprised. He arched his thick eyebrows, fiddled with his fingers, and coughed. The canal was silent, except for the light buzzing of mosquitoes.

When I finished, he looked up from his seat. "They put you in a cage? Jesus. Want me to arrest him?" His voice had changed slightly; the tone was colder.

"You could do that?"

He started up the engine while Marcus played with Cal on the floor of the boat. I swatted bugs from my face, swallowed hard. "Hey, I don't think any charges would stick," he said. "He'd be out in less than two hours, but I could arrest him if you want me to."

"I don't know. What for?"

"You'd have to sign a complaint, maybe for the money or maybe for the steroids, unless there's something else you haven't said, something else on your mind?"

I grabbed the paddle and pushed the boat off the shore while looking down into the water. The shiners had disappeared, replaced with a skin of bugs on top of the water. Dario unhinged the engine, dropped it in the water, then started it.

"I'm not sure how that would help me. I don't know."

The engine choked and sputtered. Marcus looked at his father.

"Why come to me, Legget? I mean, it's OK. I'm glad you did. But why not go to your man at the pound? Seems like they'd want to help."

"Can't do it, Dario. It's personal. I've got to solve my own problem here, you know?"

"Yeah, well, looks like you need to do something, Legget. Maybe just pull your arm back in the boat so I can get my boy home in time for dinner."

Chapter 13

I have known people who teased an animal until it turned against them. Did they expect it from the start? Seems like they did in some way, but maybe on the outside they didn't know. It felt like that with Dr. Fielding. He'd said I couldn't hurt him, and maybe he was right. The idea made my head ache. The idea of killing in such a seemingly empty way, like what happened to the animals. There had to be more to it. Maybe I was just sick of the whole thing. But I felt like I was still in it, and I was used to getting pushed around.

I rang Cathy's number for the third time, but got the answering machine. This time I left a message, not sure what to say other than telling her to stay away from Diamond for the next couple of days. I knew she couldn't, but I had to tell her. Maybe Sam would get word now, too. I grabbed my boots off the floor and wiped them with a dirty T-shirt. I'd tossed my uniform on the bed a few days ago and went back there to find it. It was twisted up in the sheets in a knot. I didn't know if it was a good idea to wear it, but I pulled it on and tucked it in tight, thinking I would try and give some official feeling to what we were about to do.

Dario had said there was a certain way to do these kinds of things, and I had to trust him. Besides, he knew about the law and I needed him on my side if things went wrong. Cal was all over my heels as I got dressed, so I sat on the couch and roughed him up a little to try and help him burn off the energy. I filled his bowls with fresh water and food, then went around the trailer once more to make sure there wasn't anything he could get into. I kept him away with my boot as I stood holding the flimsy door and reached around to shut off the lights.

I listened to him bark, then howl as I got in the Luv, and wondered how long the neighbors would put up with him. I didn't know if he barked at all noises or only when I was around. The trailer next to mine had windows covered up with tinfoil. I'd seen an old man once or twice getting into an old Chevy, but that was about all I knew of the trailer right next door. As for the others, I was sure they could hear that dog bark, and I hoped he would shut up soon, though I had a feeling he wouldn't.

The Luv sputtered when I turned the key and pumped the gas pedal. I was getting the feel of the old truck and knew how to nurse it. Dario was supposed to meet me at Roosters, a bar with a faded chicken painted on a tin roof near Diamond Kennels. It was the kind of place truckers or bikers went to, and Dario had picked it as a good place to meet, and I didn't argue. I was just glad he was helping me.

It was that time of the day when the sun was coming down and there wasn't so much traffic because it was between the time people came home from work and went out for the evening. I pulled a Sweet out and lit it with the truck lighter and put my elbow out of the open window. I liked this time and wondered if it was because I was doing what I thought was right. It felt right. But I doubted my feeling because I also had so little choice.

When I pulled into the hard-packed dirt parking lot at Roosters, I didn't see Dario's Bronco, and there were a lot of old cars in a jumble. I drove around the cars slow and looked. The porthole doors of the bar were both open, and inside I saw a red light and heard music and shouting. The bar was trying to look like a ship. I saw the outline of people in the bar and felt a wild energy from it.

I went around the lot once, spinning up yellow dust, and parked in the back away from the other cars. I stared in the rearview mirror a minute and watched the road for the Bronco, then decided to slip inside and see what was there. I was a little early.

I walked through the dust and cars to the open doors and stood a second to let my eyes adjust. There weren't as many people inside as I'd thought. The bar went back farther than I could see, and there was a cigarette machine next to me and a drunk man leaning against it with his head resting on the top. I saw the red and white package of Marlboro cigarettes in the tray at the bottom of the machine and matches, but the drunk was just leaning there. A long bar ran to the left and was scattered with beer glasses and brown bowls with peanuts or chips. Every few feet, cigarette smoke trailed up in a straight line, then into a cloud from ashtrays on the bar.

They didn't look like bikers, just hard people with hard eyes and beards and long hair and boots. A girl danced on the back part of the bar. She was barefoot and half naked, and the three or four men below her were reaching up trying to touch her and shouting and knocking each other around. I stepped in and went to the bar, where I could see the entrance and some of the parking lot.

"I just want some water," I told the bartender who came over and smiled and showed his missing front teeth. I watched the girl on the other side lift up her shirt some and roll her hips, then took the water and drank it down. My throat was dry, but my insides felt steady. I shouldn't have come into the bar, but I'd wanted to see it, and here it was. I wasn't missing anything.

Then I caught a truck out of the corner of my eye and stepped outside again to see if it was Dario. It was. He drove the Bronco around the lot, spinning up yellow dust too, then pulled in next to the Luv. I covered my mouth and walked over.

Dario hopped down from the cab. He wore black jeans and a black T-shirt and a black belt with small pouches.

"Dario," I shouted, and he turned, then waved.

"What are you doing in there?" he asked.

"Just getting some water." I clapped him on the back. "What do you want me to do?"

He turned from the cab and eyed me hard and didn't say anything. I looked in the cab at what he was fooling with and saw a shotgun with the barrel cut down and a pistol-grip handle. There were six blue shells on the seat, along with a cell phone and a gold necklace with a cross wrapped around his gear shift.

"Hop in the truck, Legget."

I got in the other side and started to think about being locked inside that cage at the farm and made myself think about the roaches skimming the top of the water and my hand moving in piss. Dario put the shotgun on the floor between the seats and climbed back in the truck. Then I thought about that hole where all the greyhounds were dead and covered over with dirt.

"You got a piece?" Dario started the truck and gunned it.

"In my truck," I said and pointed to the Luv.

"You better get it," he said and put the truck in neutral.

"You think?"

"Yeah, I think." Dario shook his head.

I jumped out, went to the Luv and grabbed the .22. Then the glove compartment wouldn't close right. I slammed it hard, but it wouldn't close, so I put the pistol down on the seat and fiddled with the latch and slammed it again. Dario moved the Bronco out of the parking slot and idled behind the Luv. I tucked the pistol in my pocket and got back in the Bronco.

"Usually don't have to lock up the truck," I said and put the pistol on the floor next to the shotgun.

"You ought to." Dario pulled onto the street. I pointed west, then gave him directions.

It wasn't so late that I didn't expect anyone to be there. With dogs, you had to be around a lot more than a regular job, and there could have been someone there. Dario didn't seem worried about it. He stopped the Bronco where the sign was stabbed into the ground. He put it in park and coughed, then reached down for the shotgun.

"Guess we're going to have to walk." Dario hooked the cell phone into the belt.

I took the pistol and got out of the truck. Dario was ahead of me, and I saw the metal shine on his handcuffs against the moonlight at the back side of his belt. The kennel was dark, but it wasn't so late. I tried to remember the last time I'd been there; I thought there were lights then. I caught up with Dario.

"Don't shoot anyone unless I tell you," Dario said.

"How do I know?"

"You'll know."

The parking lot was empty, and Dario took out a small flashlight a little bigger than a pencil and shined it over the cages. I saw the chain link fences and the nametag for Torpedo Joe, but no dogs.

"Point it to the bottom of the cages."

He pointed it, and the cage bottoms were clean, and there were no bowls of food or water.

"No water. No dogs," I said, and headed toward where the office would be.

"It doesn't matter," Dario said. "You're after the farm anyway."

I found the office and took Dario's light. Without the light I could barely see him in his dark clothes. It was quiet around the kennel, but there was noise from somewhere around it, a steady rumble of something. I couldn't say what. It had to be the farm. Then a thought came to me that shook things up. The greyhounds were seasonal; maybe they were gone, packed up everything and shipped out. That's why they let me go after locking me inside the cage.

This would be a bad mistake. It might be months before they returned. I went to the office door and turned the knob. It was locked, but it was just a knob lock because the door moved where a dead bolt would be.

"What do you think?" I asked Dario.

"Go for it."

I leaned against the door again and pushed, but it wouldn't burst open that way. So I stepped back and kicked it just behind the knob, and the door cracked. Then I leaned against it, and it opened easily.

I was thinking of what I would do if they were gone. I needed something real to put things right again. I needed to bust Dr. Fielding. He thought he was better than me, smarter. Maybe so. Maybe he could farm greyhounds, but he couldn't kill them and drop them in a hole like rats.

The office had been packed up. There was nothing on the desk. The drawers were empty. The metal folding chairs were hanging from a nail on the side wall. The small refrigerator was unplugged, with the door swinging open.

"They're gone," I said to Dario, who stood somewhere outside. No answer.

I stepped out of the office with the flashlight and pointed it around to find Dario. "Dario!"

I didn't see him, and he didn't answer. I smelled the pine trees just then, and maybe jasmine, and looked at the moon. It was half hidden by treetops. I thought it was right to come here, but why? There were different reasons in my head. I didn't know which one would be right. I wanted to put things back the way they had been. If it was for my own sake, was it the right thing to do, or was I the same as them? Maybe things couldn't go back to the way they were. Maybe they weren't supposed to.

I guessed Dario was looking around some, and I turned off the flashlight, then went through the cages toward the shed where I'd first met Cathy and where the rabbits were kept. She'd told me they were pets. I knew maybe some of them were, but some were used to train the dogs. Live lure. It didn't make sense that this would be the only kennel that had rabbits and didn't use them that way. Nothing is simple, I thought, and opened the door to the shed.

"Dario," I said once behind me and stood still and listened.

I pointed the light into the shed and it went right to the wire cages. The cages were stacked on top of another. Water bowls were wired to the part of the cage that opened. Trays slid beneath the cage bottoms which were also made of wire, so stuff would fall into the tray and you just pulled it out to clean it. No rabbits.

The place had definitely been cleaned out. But that made sense. They let me go because they were leaving. But Fielding. Fielding couldn't leave, and he never did. He had the hospital to run. There was more to it than I knew. That's why I'm here, I thought to myself and felt good. There were things I needed to know. Where the hell was Dario?

I walked around the cages once more, and he was gone. I stood in front of an empty cage and thought of what could have happened. He had to have his own plan, or maybe he thought it was better if he went on to the farm alone. I checked the pistol to make sure it was secure and went back to the office, then went around it where the aloe plants were and used the light to find the trail that was blocked by a tree stump.

After I went a short way through the trees, I saw the lights of the farm. I heard the noises I had heard before, the commotion of dogs and machines. I stopped where the path ended and saw the farm ahead of me. The two floodlights lit the cages where the dogs moved. I saw the bulldozer parked just beyond the cages. I remembered where the hole had been dug and drew a path in my mind as best I could in the dark areas outside of the farm to get closer. I wondered what I was supposed to do now without Dario.

Punk trees guarded the farm buildings from sight if you weren't close, and I crouched at the edge of these trees and made my way around. I looked for the Mexicans but saw no one, not even Dario. The place had a kind of shut-down look and I didn't expect what happened.

Another building stood across from the kennel with a sidewalk between. It had no cages that I could see and looked like a building for people. I watched this building. A window on the left side had light coming out that flickered, and I guessed there were people moving inside. The window was too high for it to be the movement of animals.

Then I saw him. Dr. Fielding opened a door that faced the sidewalk and yellow light flooded the area, and I saw him standing there with his hand on the doorknob. He leaned out and studied the darkness. He didn't say anything or shout for whoever he was looking for, but stood and moved his head from left to right. He shut the door, and I caught his voice saying words to someone in the building.

I took the pistol from my pocket and sat on the dirt and dead leaves. I could wait. But I would be waiting a long time, and for what? Dario was gone. But he hadn't just disappeared. He was down there, and they were waiting for me. I knew this. It had been coming to this, and now it was here. I stood, brushed the dirt from my pants, and worked my shirt around straight and put the pistol down the front of my pants with the handle out.

I didn't try and hide or walk quietly, but went straight down and came near the cages, and the dogs turned or opened their eyes and enough barked that they would hear inside the building and know I was coming. I walked through the soft dirt at the backs of the cages and looked at the eyes of the animals, like deer or children. I thought if I could do anything, I could help these animals; then I found myself in front of the door. The smell of animal shit was strong, and it was night but it was still hot and the air was heavy. I heard my heart in my ears when the dogs went quiet.

Taking the pistol out, I pointed it straight and opened the door. There was a long hallway with one door at the end of a larger room. I saw bags that looked like flour sacks stacked on the floor. In the hallway the ceiling was high and the light was enough to see, but not bright. There were shadows and a metal chair close to the door.

"Dario," I shouted.

I knew they would try and kill me. Fielding had more than the farm to protect. He had the hospital, a reputation. And Dario had involved himself the first time, at the Holton house. The Holton house, where it started. There was something there, too. Well if I was going to die, I would die. I wasn't running away. I rubbed my eyes and felt tired. Just let it be fast with no way out and I will just accept it. But I didn't want it that way. I put the pistol in my pants again. I couldn't win like that.

The door at the far end of the hallway opened and Dario was standing there. I saw the shotgun pointing in the air and bright steel reflections behind him.

"Come on, Legget."

"What's happening, Dario?"

"Come on," Dario said again and shut the door.

I walked to the door and thought of Cathy and Cal and John. I didn't want to die. But I'm walking right into it, I thought and wondered if I would always be a fool.

I opened the door and right away got hit in the eyes with a blinding light. I caught the shape of a light I had seen before over surgery tables in animal hospitals and put my hands to my eyes and could not see. I was pulled into the room and shoved face against the wall. The wall was covered with cold tiles and hard against my teeth.

"All right," I said.

"Listen to me, Legget." It was Dr. Fielding. The light was hot against my back.

"I'm listening."

"I don't want to kill you, Legget."

"You fuck with my life. What's the difference?"

"See what I mean," Fielding said to someone else, maybe Dario. Then I felt the barrel end of a gun at my neck and could hear the breaths close by.

"I can honestly say I thought you'd just move on to something else. What's an ACO make? Fifteen, twenty?"

"I never thought about it," I said trying to figure out Fielding's logic. He thought I'd scare off, but it had never occurred to me to let this go. I was proud suddenly of something inside me I hadn't seen before. "Let me turn around. What's the difference," I said and started to turn when the barrel pressed hard into my ear.

"Let the hero turn around," Fielding ordered.

He leaned his tall body into a surgery table and moved the overhead light against the other wall. The walls were white tiles and clean, and the room was bright. Dario stood next to Fielding. His face showed nothing. I was betrayed, and his face showed nothing but that hard, straight look a cop can have that means things can go either way, and either way you will not win.

"You can't start over now, Legget." Fielding pushed his glasses up.

To me, he looked the same. The good doctor. He'd been kind to animals and to me; he seemed to love them, but who was this man? So I didn't know everything.

"You can't kill a man like you kill these dogs. Someone's gonna find out what happens here," I said and kept my eyes on the doctor. I didn't want to look at Dario.

"I can do it if I want to, Legget. You think I'm going to let you screw up my business, lose my license because of some feeling you have for these dogs? Big problem," he said and looked at his nails.

"What difference does it make to you? You've got everything you need."

"It makes a difference. Things aren't as simple as you make them. You must know that by now."

"Maybe you never wanted me to stop. Maybe you can't stand your own skin."

I watched his eyes dart up from his long fingers and I saw the white eyebrows with long hairs that twined behind his glasses.

"Why hurt these dogs, Fielding?" I shouted.

"Because I can," he said.

Dario moved his hand. I wasn't looking at him, but I could see the movement. I just caught a flash of color near my eyes and felt a cold rush through my chest and in my head, and I was thinking about those dogs and what they were doing to them and how it could all stop, and maybe it couldn't after all, no matter what I did.

I spat blood on the clean floor and held my gut and looked at Fielding again. If he was going to kill me, I'd make him look me in the eye.

"Kill him in the field," Fielding said in a flat voice, then dropped his leg from the table and moved for the door.

Dario stepped forward, shoved the barrel into my back and pushed.

"Let's go," he said and pushed again.

I stepped to the door and pushed it open, knowing this was it. This was going to be my last chance to get away. Just me and Dario, but he was a cop and knew how to handle someone.

"Keep walking," he said as I turned on to the grass and headed out into the darkness of the field.

I turned my head to see his face and where he was standing.

"Turn around," Dario shouted. The fucking coward couldn't look at me.

But he was too far back for me to turn around and fight him for the gun, and we were deeper in the field and I couldn't think of what to do. The sky seemed low and blue-black and stuffed with stars. If I ran he'd have an easy shot. The trees and cover were too far. Then I felt something in my shoulders, like an urge that came from nowhere, and I turned again at the same second Dario cursed and stumbled over something in the grass. My legs exploded with energy as I moved after him, and watched the barrel of the gun fall to a bead on the ground, then lift again as Dario righted himself.

Rushes of wind carried me around the arms when my fist flung out for that piece of flesh in his face that light speckled and drew me toward. It was a flash of a second and I heard the soft splatter of bone and felt the warm blood and heard the grunt of air and pain that welled up from him. I could think of nothing but the trees and cover and kept running with the same motion of the punch and ran hard feeling in my mind the sight of that barrel at my back like a cold finger.

Then there was the pop of the shotgun and the spray of pellets slapping against the leaves and trees in front of me. I cut left, then left again and dove for the trees knocking my teeth against the ground and roots. But my blood pumped hard in my ears and there was no pain. I lifted myself and ran again, dodging tree trunks and bushes and hedges like a hundred Darios in the moonlight.

My lungs burned and the trees thinned, and through the dark I thought I saw a road or a clear space ahead. I couldn't run anymore. I tried to pump my legs and felt blood or sweat on my right thigh and wiped my hands on my shirt and started looking for cover.

I was at the edge of the trees and saw a ditch and then the highway, but no cars. I ducked back into the trees and saw a clump of low palm scrub and headed for it, then ducked and crawled beneath the fronds. I pulled my legs into the little grove of palm and laid my head on my arm and took deep breaths and closed my eyes. I heard noises all around me and knew Dario would be looking for me, but I had to stop and think and catch my wind.

Chapter 14

I crawled through soft dirt under the trees and rolled over and I was near the street. Cars came at me with their headlights blazing. It all looked strange and close from the ground, and I rolled again but realized I wasn't so close to the road unless a car swerved. A pulsing in my head; I thought this must be what it's like to get kicked by a horse. I tried to remember Fielding and what he'd said, and I was alive.

After my head, I felt pain in my right hand and moved it near my face to try and look at it when a car passed. Then a car came and I heard the roar of the tires sucking the road and saw my best two fingers were broken. Those bastards couldn't kill me, I thought, and put the hand down and stared at the sky and tried to catch my wind. I tried to guess how long I'd been in the scrub. An hour?

I was never much for stars, but then, looking up and seeing so many, I thought they might stop the pain in my head and fingers, and I wondered if there was someone up there guiding me along. Maybe that was the only reason I wasn't dead: so there were things left for me to do.

I pulled myself up and started walking along the road toward the carnival of jittering traffic lights and street lamps. It was easy to see why people just worried about themselves and why things like this could happen in secret. It was all for money and the struggle of doing what you thought you had to do. I wasn't much different.

The lights from the 7-Eleven were warm, and the smell of roasting hot dogs and car exhaust, beer, and old trash cans kept me awake. I found a spot against the railing at the side of the building and leaned. I watched people go in and out of the store. I supposed I looked like a vagrant and wondered if the clerks would come out and roust me. But I was on the side of the building, out of the light, beneath the shadow.

I fought an urge to fall asleep, then realized I'd been there too long. They'd be looking for me, and I couldn't be too far from the farm. I went inside and walked over to the roasting hot dogs and smelled them as my stomach turned over. I saw the bathroom, on the other side of an ice machine and a bucket of dirty mop water, and headed for it. After closing the door, I sat on the toilet seat and studied my hand.

The fingers were twisted backwards some and still throbbed, but I was getting used to it. I bit down and closed my eyes and grabbed the fingers with my left hand and got in where I could feel the little bones sticking out. I pushed them down while pulling the fingers back straight. They cracked, and I was nauseated and the throbbing picked up so much I turned the water on at the sink, trying to get it cold, but there was only lukewarm water. I let it run over my hand, stream between the fingers and back down to the sink. I watched the dirt and dried blood fall into the white bowl, and resisted the urge to look at my face.

But I did look, and other than a streak of road dirt acoss my cheek and the darkness around my eyes, I looked the same. Funny, but I didn't look at myself too much, and here it was. Brown eyes staring back at me. I could almost be a stranger. I tore a piece of rough paper from the dispenser and wetted it, and tried to clean the dirt with my left hand and look in the mirror. But it was too much with everything backwards and opposite.

I went to the register, where the clerk fidgeted like he was on a coke high, with his arms twitching and hands that couldn't keep still. I looked into his blue eyes.

"Give me a quarter," I said.

And he popped open the register and handed it over. Must be the uniform, I thought, and dropped it in my pocket and went outside.

I could think of only one person who might help me set things somewhere close to normal, and I wasn't too sure he'd want to talk. I eyed the two phones and figured old friends would always listen no matter what had happened up to then. I wanted someone who knew me and could think past the problems. So I found his number in a phone book that was swelled up with water and tried to think of how to explain it all.

"It's Legget." I heard John sucking at a cigar and blowing the smoke out slow, which meant he was thinking hard. I imagined him sitting at the kitchen table in a T-shirt, a bottle of scotch nearby.

"Yeah?"

"I need some help. They tried to kill me."

"I don't sound surprised do I?"

"No." I didn't think Leland could be so cold.

"Why don't you talk to the police?"

"The cops are bad. I can't go that way. I need your help."

"I don't know." I heard him suck at that cigar again. I knew he wasn't going to make things too easy.

"She's letting you do that in the house now?"

"She's out playing Canasta tonight."

"Oh, yeah? If I could tell you what's happening, John, you might think different."

"I might."

"Maybe you could meet me at Greenhorns in the morning? I could tell you what's what and then you decide. I can't talk too much right now."

He was quiet for what seemed like a long time as I stared at the blue wall of the 7-Eleven, then pulled the phone close and squeezed my shoulders between the phone and the casing, hoping no one was watching.

"There's one thing, Legget."

"Name it." I swallowed. He seemed so far away through the phone.

"You got to do things my way. No matter what. I'm not discussing this, I'm telling you."

"I can do that, John. I can." I felt a whole wave of relief and anxiety slip away for a moment; then it came back just as fast and settled in my gut.

"Say nine?"

"OK, I'll be there."

"All right."

"Thanks, John."

"All right now."

I was ashamed of what I'd done on the body tour, enough to make me try and work things out alone. I could see him in that old kennel way—with a rifle and that kind of spooked look in his eyes and all the dead greyhounds, and I thought maybe he still had it in him. If he didn't, I had nowhere else to go.

If it took me twenty minutes to drive from Diamond to the trailer, I figured it would take an hour or two to walk it. Going around the backs of buildings and through alleys and dark streets was just my thing, like I was catching dogs. And I could keep out of sight. Maybe Dario could put the word out to the sheriffs to pick me up on some charge that wasn't true. Or maybe they'd prefer to handle it themselves. Either way, someone was looking for me, and they'd be in a hurry now.

So I started walking, talking deep breaths and watching every which way for blue flashes and cars slowing down. I ducked behind the pool supply store, then behind a whole row of shops in a strip mall and stayed away from the flood lights bouncing off the stark back walls. It was an ugly town, I thought, from the back side, but I was also drawn to it, like it was part of my nature to creep beneath and behind what everyone else was supposed to see on the fronts of things.

* * *

Later, I found myself in the woods behind the trailer park and stayed low, trying to catch a glimpse of my trailer and whatever cars were around it. It wouldn't be hard for Dario to figure where I lived and just sit there and wait for me. But it looked the same, from where I stood behind a pine tree. I put my hands on the trunk and felt my pulse between the thumb and the rough skin of the tree.

My luck was on, I thought, because I still had the pistol tucked in my pants. But I hoped I wouldn't use it. I just had to find a way around the ditch that ran behind the trailers, get to the street and weave back to mine. But it was dark and the ditch was steep. I worked my way down and jumped over the trickle of water that went through, then climbed up the other side and crouched. I needed to get Cal, get my hands on him and keep him safe before they came.

I walked up the street, but stayed away from the yards in case a dog jumped out or someone thought I was a thief. The parked cars and lights and sounds were the same as always. I wondered if I was still lucky and had beat Dario. But I thought they would come no matter what. And how could I prove that he'd tried to kill me? There was no way I could prove it. My word against his was a sure loser. When I got to my trailer, I walked around and looked through the windows. I wanted to see if Cal would hear me and bark, and if there was anyone inside. It was dark inside and I could hear nothing. But Cal was in there and he didn't bark. So I couldn't count on him to guard us. I went around to the kitchen window and poked at the screen a little. Then I heard Cal bump the kitchen table and grumble, but no bark.

"Hey, Cal," I said and saw his head with his ears pricked up.

There couldn't be anyone in there if Cal would just run to the window, so I went around and opened the door and Cal burst out and went sniffing right away. He pissed heavy on the cover of the electric stump in the front yard. I went there and touched his head and felt a fear along my back as if someone, maybe Dario, would appear. I didn't want to chase the dog, but he must be crazy from sitting inside the trailer for so long. When he was done, I pulled him back and took him inside and found a choker to walk him. I arranged the pistol and put my shirt over it and locked the door.

Even though I wanted nothing more than to shower and sleep I shook it off and took Cal around the back way of the park and let him sniff around and stretch his legs. How was it I could walk through the park with people living normal lives while they hunted me? You saw the lights and the televisions' glow and heard kids and wondered what was real. But Cal was safe, and John would help, and I only had to make it through to the morning.

I found bread in the fridge and sat on the couch with all the lights off. Cal sat next to me and I fed him some bread and put my arm over his chest. I ate the bread, then found cheese and cut a thick slice and ate that too. I didn't know a man could be so hungry. Sitting on the couch made the pains in my fingers return, and I tried to remember if I had anything to take for it, but I didn't want to get up from the couch again.

I checked the pistol and made sure it was ready and put it on the arm of the couch and thought about Fielding. So everyone in the business knew that he'd struggled with the way things had changed. The old vets knew farms and livestock and rubber boots. The new vets knew blood tests and grooming and dog shows. The new vets stole the clients and Dr. Fielding had less and less. And then he would lose the status he'd worked so hard for. But he'd had status with men like me until things fell apart. People like John and me and other ACOs knew how he could see the illness in an animal with his hands. I wondered why that wasn't enough. But it must be the drinking, I thought.

Ever since the first day I met him he was a drinker, and then there was this Crystal K.

I've known of vets who would take the drugs from their hospital for a cold or flu or an allergy. That made sense. And why wouldn't he try a little of this to sleep or to calm down and then it happened? People got hooked and couldn't stop. It was in the blood somehow, and I didn't understand much more than that.

So he would kill me because I would destroy what was left. He could make the choices about covering up a murder. He needed power. Power over the farm and Sam and the Mexicans. Just like the farm I grew up on. I remembered people who needed power, control over others like the migrant workers, and nothing more. He had to kill me because I would turn things inside out and everyone would see what he was really about.

I thought of Dr. Diaz when I was a boy and could see his face and the red vein that stood out in his eye when he looked at me. That man had balanced the power inside him. I knew there was something there, something to learn. I felt I was close to it now, and would figure it out if I lived. Cal got up and paced the floor like he wanted to go out again and I settled him. I checked the windows and saw nothing and wondered if they would come. None of this would have happened if I'd been loyal to Fielding. But I couldn't be a part of what they did to those dogs.

Then Cal gave up and huffed and sauntered toward the bedroom, where he liked to sleep on the floor. I took the pistol in my good hand and put it on my chest. I started to think of what to say to John and how he could help set things straight. And I saw Dr. Diaz again and the farm where I grew up and could almost hear his voice, but not enough to know the words. Then Dr. Diaz turned into Dr. Fielding and he was white and stumbling and I heard him say, "Kill him in the field." Then I knew I was falling asleep and shook it off, but stayed where I was and let my thoughts drift.

I saw the farm at Diamond Kennel as if I were in the trees. There were greyhounds huddled together, maybe twenty in the field, and the bulldozer and Sam tying them together with rope. But behind this I saw orange light flickering between dark patches and heard barking. There was something familiar to the barking and it kept pulling me away from the greyhounds, but I couldn't figure where. I felt the heat of the Palm County sun and started to sweat, and the flickering was heavy, like when your eyes are closed and you look at the sky.

* * *

Then something made me open my eyes and Cal was there, staring me in the face, and nothing was right. I heard the crackling of the fire that roared from the back of the trailer like a storm, and Cal was burned. But I was shaking off the sleep and panicked and stood and didn't know what to do. I clutched the pistol, knowing I couldn't let it go. The fire was heavy in the kitchen and black soot came in waves. I put my shirt to my mouth and went to the door. I kicked the door and could feel the heat through my boot, but it didn't open. The windows in the room were too small to get through and the fire was coming closer. Cal barked and jumped at me and I saw again somehow he was burned and his eyes looked yellow.

The heat was plastic and full of acid. It filled my nose and head and throat with this acid taste, choking me, cutting off the good air. I couldn't see anything but waves and little bands of heat and heard Cal's wailing. I kicked at the door again, but it only buckled. Someone must have blocked it, I realized. Cal had run through the fire in the kitchen and was barking somewhere behind it. Then I realized the window in the bedroom was big enough. Maybe the dog was telling me. Cal came running through the fire again and ran into me, barking in my face.

I pushed him back and yelled and he went through the flames again and I followed him to the bedroom. I wasn't thinking anymore and grabbed Cal by the chest and felt his loose, wet skin and heaved him through the window. The glass broke and the dog went flying through, spinning like he was trying to stand up in the air. It didn't look real. I dove through the window and felt the air outside and fell into the ditch and rolled. But my blood pumped hard and I lifted and looked for the dog. He had told me what to do and figured it out faster.

Then I saw the trailer, metal panels bubbling red and white, black smoke thick as mud billowing off the edges. The blurred lines of door and window and yard and sky. A small crowd stood out in the street, in bathrobes, pointing fingers, a quick bustling of confused minds, not knowing what to do.

I ran into the trees looking for the dog. Cal was in there somehwere and wailing like I'd never heard an animal wail. Something snapped in my head; it felt like a tight band running down my neck was stretched too far and snapped. I could hear it, or maybe it was blood pounding in my ears, and it hurt.

Cal darted past me, his fur smoking and charred, and I followed him to the front where the crowd was and where I finally caught him in my burned arms. But Cal was worse off than me. His skin was black and pink, his fur singed, skin bleeding white and yellow, bubbling sores along his back. He barked and yelped as I picked him up, scooping his legs in my arms like I knew to do and pulling him close. His body was so hot. It burned my chest too. I wanted to draw him in and take the pain away. Give it to me, I thought. Give me the pain, but Cal had it and it made him bite, flipping his head back and what was left of his ears hitting me in the face.

I turned and saw the people and trailer behind the waves of heat. I carried Cal into a yard, struggling against me and put him on the ground near the passenger door of a truck. I heard a woman screaming from behind and sirens emerging from deep within the heart of Palm County.

"I got to do it now," I said sing-song and quiet to Cal, who struggled under my boot. My mouth trembled. The sting in my eyes was tears and smoke. I knew it was the best way. I couldn't stand to listen to his howls. And he was my dog. No one else could do it. He'd been burned more because he'd kept running through the fire to get me, to wake me up.

Two shots through his little skull put an end to it. My eyes burned. I felt the sores puckering on my chest, my arms, my hands blistering where I held the pistol. Maybe I felt the dog's pain leaking out, oozing into me, and I wanted it. Cal's body was still. A fire truck pulled into the little street and moved the crowd. I stood above Cal like a statue. I heard someone saying something behind me, but I wasn't there. I looked at the sky and retreated into my mind and could see only one thing.

Dr. Fielding. I felt the howl coming. A wave swirling fast like a hurricane and building—up my legs, my heart, my throat, then finally exploding from my flung mouth.

I started walking. I only wanted to walk away and find quiet. I found myself on the sidewalk outside the park, and though I could still hear the noise of the fire and sirens, ahead it looked clear. So I walked toward town, thinking that by the time I got there it would be morning and John would come, and I had to think until then of what I could do.

Chapter 15

For a second, I could pretend things were back to normal when I saw John in his pressed uniform. He sat in the booth with his phone propped up and a scattering of papers across the table and a pot of coffee and even two cups. I had found a spigot outside and cleaned up some. I got a sick feeling and knew I still looked like shit, but maybe that would help my case.

I slipped into the booth, grabbed a coffee cup and saw Rita glance over from the waitresses' island, and poured coffee while watching the steam curl up and float away. If I let Cal slip into my mind I would lose control. I felt John's staring and didn't look till I got the burn on my tongue from the coffee and swallowed. I took a deep breath. A little sun was coming through the window, making lines on the table and John's papers.

I let the familiar sounds of plates and water glasses and the conversations filter in and settle my head down. I could have just exploded, not knowing what would come out of my mouth, but I didn't. I held it in.

"Legget, you look like hell," John finally said and clicked the button on his pen.

I looked up and felt a flush of guilt run through my throat. "Yeah,

I didn't plan it this way."

"Wouldn't think so."

"I almost don't know what to say, don't want to screw this up you know."

"Don't worry about it. Give me the short."

When Rita came over, I smelled the pancakes on her. I told her I was fine with just coffee though my stomach was grumbling. John did the same.

"OK," I said. "My trailer's burned. Someone torched it last night while I was in it. I know that Dr. Fielding sells greyhounds upstate, to the University I think, probably for medical research, shit like that. It's a breeding farm, mid-size. And Dario, you know the sheriff, he's in on it too. I found out the hard way. I found a grave. Big damned hole filled with dogs, and there's old rope. I know they tied them up and pulled them. Starved the ones that won't race or were going to bury them alive. I went there to see it for myself, but they caught me and Dario, Jesus, Dario took me out into the field ..."

"All right." I watched John nod, look down at his papers, then look me in the eyes. Maybe he was looking for some sign that I was telling the truth.

"And what do you want out of this? What I mean is: you know how hard it is to bust these guys. And Fielding's a vet. Hell."

"The farm! Jesus! That's not the point. He was gonna shoot me. Besides, we got the rope. That's easy cruelty. He'd lose his license, everything." I felt my fingers pulse hard, and I squeezed the leg of the table like an arm.

"Hey! Goddamn it, Legget, I know the point," John said and

glanced around to see if he'd attracted attention.

"OK, OK, John. I know," I said in a hushed voice. "Just listen to me, I'm in this deep shit. I got no way out. Where am I going to go?"

"All right, take it easy, Legget. I understand. Let's just cool down." John pulled his coffee close and blew at the top.

Rita walked by and eyed me as if we'd better cool down too, and I looked out the window and saw two sheriff's cars, and a bolt of fear went through me, thinking it was Dario.

"I just want things to go back to the way they were. I'm no hero. I want to catch dogs, drive the streets. Hell, I'll clean cages if I have to, if you'll help me, John."

John nodded and sipped his coffee and moved his head, urging me to take a drink too. He picked up the phone and tested its weight. I saw him thinking and kept my mouth full of coffee so I wouldn't say anything else. The sheriff walked in and it wasn't Dario.

"I got someone I can call," John said.

"Does he owe you a favor?"

"I wouldn't say that."

The busboy wheeled by, clanking dishes and glasses in his cart. I could see the inside of the cart where all the leftover egg pieces and waffles and syrup and ice were thrown from empty tables. It had a strong, bad smell, and I nodded to myself.

"You know how much ..."

"I know," John interrupted. "You don't deserve to go through all this, Legget. Maybe we can fix things, just drain the whole situation like a beer with a hole in the can, huh?" John lifted his eyebrows like a question.

"OK," I said and chuckled as John stood up with the phone and walked over to the lobby, waving me to stay put and wait.

I watched John pace the carpeted floor in shiny boots, talking on the phone to someone on the other end that I could never talk to, and maybe for him it was one call he could make in his whole life and that would be it. I didn't know how to pay him back.

"Let's go," John said and reached across the table and swiped his papers into a pile, then tucked them under his arm.

There were a lot of reasons for me to go and keep my mouth shut and do what John told me. But I needed to know he was in it for me and not just half-assed.

"Where?" I said.

"What?" John looked surprised. Stood there with his hand in midair holding a dollar bill tip.

"What's the plan?" I stayed in the booth, sitting, avoiding his eyes then thought better and looked right at him.

"They really tried to kill you?"

"John, it was pure dumb luck they're not feeding me to the greyhounds right now."

He nodded and slipped back into the booth, dropped his papers on the table again.

"I'm not saying I can solve all this, Legget. But I'm with you, OK? Killing goes way past what you did on the body tour. You understand? We go back farther than that. You're back in with us now," he rolled his fingers over the shiny ACO badge pinned to his shirt. "OK?"

"OK," I said and let out a lungful of air and took his hand in a shake that sealed it for me.

"Why don't you hit the washroom? I have a clean shirt in the truck. Let's go."

I smelled my own sweat in the close, hot cab of John's truck. I pulled off my shirt as he turned the ignition, then gunned the engine. I felt the vibration of the clutch through my boots in the dark floorboards.

"Hey, open that glovebox," John said and gunned the engine again.

I opened the box with my good, left hand and looked inside.

"Is it in there?"

I watched him glance in the side mirror, bobbing his head up and down to see something.

"You mean this?" I tossed the bad shirt on the floorboard and pulled out a .45. It was a heavy pistol, and I moved it in my palm so the grip was right.

"Yeah, let's see it." John took the pistol and popped the magazine and glanced in. I saw the brass rounds with blunt tips and nodded to myself while pulling the clean shirt around my shoulders.

The engine clanked and died. John handed me the .45.

"See something back there?" I started buttoning the shirt.

"No, you got me nervous." John ran his fingers over his grizzled hair then turned the ignition and gunned it hard again. "Can't count on this fucking machine much. Put that thing back in the box. OK?"

"OK," I said and thought it was better not to mention I still had the .22 pistol.

The county courthouse had been a hotel when Palm County was nothing but a fishing camp. Since then, they had added a dome and trimmed out the building's windows, painted it with pastel colors that were typically Florida. You could see the walls outside the compound sweat in the summer. The cool marble floors beyond the steps shimmered beneath the waves of warm air that blew in from antique fans oscillating at the tops of black iron poles.

I followed John down the corridor and avoided the eyes of workers and lawyers in button-up shirts with rolled sleeves and ties. I'd never liked the place. Always felt like I didn't belong around the courtrooms and water fountains and fast-walking clerks.

John walked slow, checking the brass nameplates at the sides of doors, then shrugging and moving along like he'd been here before, which I knew he had.

"Who we looking for?" I asked.

"Judge Watson."

We turned a corner into a wide hallway with oil paintings of all the old judges lining the walls and little brass lamps above them, and nameplates. Dust swirled in the heavy air toward the ceiling which was checkered with parquet tiles.

"This is it." John headed toward the middle door, motioning me to a polished wooden bench leaning up against the wall.

"Sit tight for a minute. I'll go in and talk with him; maybe he'll want to talk to you, maybe not. I don't know. Don't worry about it."

I nodded and took a seat, fighting an urge for a Sweet and a cool glass of water. I settled into the hard wood as best I could and dug my boot toes into the marble floor to keep from sliding from the polished seat. The door where John disappeared clicked shut with an empty clap. I was sure we'd passed a water fountain just before the hallway and glanced there, wondering if I should get up.

Maybe this was all it would take, I thought. I imagined that John went in and told this Judge Watson we'd been having some problems, and the old judge, if he was old, nodded and chewed his pen and made a call or just smiled and took care of it. I had no idea how that could be. Even a judge was on the outside of all this. But maybe this judge could call a cease fire, just stop everything where it stood right then.

I eased up from the bench and wandered down the hall a few steps while listening for the judge's door to open, and then went up the hallway to find the water fountain. When I turned the corner, I glanced back, satisfied I could still hear them, and looked for it.

The cool water dribbled down my chin and circled the green-crusted drain and emptied slow. I closed my eyes and followed the cool water down my throat and felt it swish around in my stomach. It had been one long goddamn night, long enough to make me wish I'd never known about Diamond Kennel. But they had pulled me as hard as I had pushed.

I stretched out my sore fingers and turned around and saw him standing at the end of the hallway in uniform, his white shirt starched and his badge gleaming gold and silver. I felt a flash of cold fear squeeze through me. Dario saw me too. It was hard to see his eyes from there, but they were killer's eyes and I couldn't forget them. I watched him flip the case of his cell phone and press the button with his thumb, not taking those cool eyes off me the whole while.

I walked back to the judge's hallway, wiping water from my chin, saw it was empty, and went straight to Judge Watson's door. Pulling the door open, I caught a rush of cold air and the smell of cherry tobacco and heard the click of computer keys. I was standing in a little reception area formed by blue, modular walls. A woman with dirty blonde hair in a bun pinned together with what looked like chopsticks stopped her typing and looked at me from over the tops of her glasses.

"Yes?"

"Judge Watson. Big black man. Where are—" I was cut off by the sound of John's voice coming from behind the cube. I saw the top of a mahogany door open.

"Legget?" John appeared from behind the secretary's walls. "What's going on?"

"Dario! He saw me. Just now. Shit, John."

"Take it easy. Legget, this is Judge Watson."

Judge Watson's shoulders almost touched each side of the door frame. He wore a grey beard and half-sized reading glasses. The judge almost had a comical look on his face, with his eyebrows raised and thick fingers pulling at his belt loop.

"I'll be waiting to hear from you, John. Nice to meet you, son."

The judge clapped John on the back, eyed me quickly and turned back to his office. John, almost bowing to the man, backed out and waved good-bye.

"Let's go," John said and ushered me out of the office.

In the hallway, John wiped a light coat of sweat from his forehead and flung it on the ground.

"Damn, almost lost it at the end there. Now what's the deal? Did he say anything to you?"

"No, he saw me, then made a call. What did the judge say?"

John rolled his eyes and started down the hallway. "Come on," he said and tugged my shoulder. "Legget, you know how things have always been with Animal Control."

"I know," I said and watched for Dario as we came out of the hallway.

"Dario isn't gonna do shit here, not with both of us," John said. "Come on."

We went outside the courthouse into the sun and John shielded his eyes and turned. "Basically he said, prove it. Now that's not so bad. Prove it and he'll prosecute this time. You hear me?"

I heard, but was looking around for Dario. John didn't seem to think about the fact that Dario was a killer. "It's there. Just have to dig them up, take some pictures," I said. "Even if Dario calls Sam, they won't have enough time to hide those poor dogs."

"Then let's get moving," John said and headed for the truck.

If the truck hadn't started the first time, I might have jumped and run. I had a feeling of the worst kind. I didn't really believe in the judge. Anytime Animal Control had ever been involved with a court case or with budget meetings or anything like it, John had complained, the veins in his neck jumping and ticking. So why was this any different? I didn't really believe in the judge, and I definetely didn't believe he could do anything fast.

"Let's go, John," I said and pushed my good hand against the dashboard as if to push the thing along.

"Did Dario say something to you?"

"Didn't have to. What makes you think this judge can do anything for me in five minutes, if at all?"

"Look at it this way, Legget. What choice do we have? Besides, he asked me about this lady Holton. Remember her? She's Fielding's ex-wife. That's Dr. Fielding. Shit, I even called him about the case. No wonder he said not to worry about it."

"So maybe she wasn't crazy. Maybe someone did break in. Explains why Dario would call me knowing it was a signal 7. It was set up from the start. They played me."

John turned the truck onto the highway and I held the door frame. So they had picked me from the start, thinking I wouldn't say anything. Fielding's body tour had me hooked, and when he wasn't sure if I'd keep my mouth shut, he'd made the call that got me fired. He'd played John too. I wondered if John realized that yet.

"Left on Superior," I said.

John took a left, then grabbed the CB and got Molly Phelps. "Listen close, Molly," he said. I saw the turn off for Diamond Kennels ahead and wondered if Dario would be waiting, or Sam, and then I thought about Cathy and hoped she was long gone.

John drove slow. I couldn't see any cars in the place where they'd parked before. I took the .45 from the glovebox and held the barrel and passed it to John. I took the .22 out of my belt and held it up, and John noticed but didn't say anything.

"Should we wait for Block?" I asked. John had called for more ACOs to come to Diamond, and Block was the closest. It would take him fifteen minutes.

"Looks like we can't. Look at this."

I looked where John pointed; a kennel truck was coming up a road behind the compound. I had never seen the trucks come from there and realized it must be where they came in and out of the farm. The truck kicked up dust, and I watched the tree shadows and sun play over the topper like a wheel.

"We're going to take this head-on, Legget," John said and turned hard.

He headed straight for the kennel truck.

"If they jump out and come this way, get out of the truck. Don't get caught in the cab. OK?"

"I'm ready," I said.

Then John turned in front of the kennel truck, which was only thirty feet away on the little dirt road and had no way of getting past us because of the heavy trees on both sides. Not even enough room to turn around. I heard the kennel truck engine gun and rev like it missed a gear; I looked through the windshield to see who drove. But the sun was bright which made the glass dark on the inside, and I couldn't see.

John honked and drove down on them slow. The kennel truck drove backward slow, too, and it was a stalemate. But we were moving forward.

"What's the plan?" I asked.

John spit out the window and sat up in the seat. "I'm not holding anybody. You got that? If they run, let them run. We'll let the sheriff catch 'em. We're going to find that hole and dig it up. When Block gets here we'll take pictures."

I took the CB and got Block and told him where to drive when he got there. Then the kennel truck sped up, tried to spin around but hit the back end of a tree. I watched the cab door burst open and saw Sam, his red hair a blaze in the light. Sam reached in and pulled a shotgun from the front seat. Like he was moving in slow motion, I watched him bear down on us with the gun while John reversed.

We both ducked beneath the dash and the shot came and ripped through the front of the truck like a fist. I heard the broken glass fall on the seat and dash like sand. John kicked open his door and rolled out, and I heard him fire, then I backed out and looked under the door to see what was what, but Sam was already gone, so I stood, and John stood too.

"You all right?" he asked.

"Fine. I told you they were serious."

John nodded. "Come on. They know we're coming."

There was nothing better than to feel my boots crunch in the dirt and leaves, to feel myself on the ground and moving. I stopped at the kennel truck and looked in the cages. There were dogs in the cages with their muzzles on and doe eyes looking out between the thin, steel bars. So Sam had figured it was time to hit the road. The season was almost over, and he was probably heading for another track to race the dogs and wait till things cooled down. But now he knew we were after him, and I wondered if Cathy was at the farm too. I didn't know what I would do.

John walked out in front slow, and we stayed to the side of the road near the oak trees and palm scrub kicking up the dead brown leaves and grey sand. I saw the farm ahead, and we were on the far side of the field where I knew the dogs were buried. It was the opposite side from where I'd run when Dario had missed his big chance. I caught up to John, who huddled behind a palm hammock.

"We can find the hole by the soft dirt, but we're in the open," I said and pointed to where I thought the hole was. "See anybody?"

John shook his head no and scratched his cheek with the pistol. "Shit, I don't think they'll shoot us. Probably rock salt in that shotgun. Just trying to scare us off is all they're doing."

"I don't know, John." I guessed the farm was far enough away that a shotgun wouldn't be too accurate if I stayed low. "Don't have the shovel anyway. We need to wait for Block."

John was quiet a minute, and my neck started to sweat. I could feel the sweat drizzling down my back.

"Doesn't matter," John said. "When Block gets here, we have the same problem. They just sit over there and shoot at us. No. We've got to clear them out before we dig."

"How do we do that?" I asked and slapped a mosquito that found my wet neck.

"Come on," John said and ducked into the trees and crouched.

I followed him through the trees, toward the kennel and the buildings and could see nothing through the movement of dogs. Before I could focus, we were there. John was breathing heavy, wiping the sweat from his neck and looking through the trees.

"I don't see anybody," I said.

John nodded. "They're there," he said and burst out of the trees.

He ran toward the chain link cages, and I knew he couldn't get through without going around the backs. I followed. John ran ahead with the .45 extended, about ten feet, maybe more, in front of me.

His boots fell heavily in the soft dirt behind the cages. Then I saw her through the chain links. She was bending down, her long hair covering her arm.

"John," I shouted, knowing she would hear me.

Then John started shouting at Cathy to step into the open, and I ran harder. "Cathy," I yelled. "It's me, come out!" But John was at the opening and I was there a moment later.

Cathy was standing with one open hand in the air, and in the other she held a choker with Torpedo Joe on the other end. John pointed the pistol at her.

"John, it's cool, put the pistol down," I said.

But Cathy was shaking her head no, her eyes wide and wild. "No," she said, waving us back. "No," she said again.

It was too late. Sam busted out of the door where Dario had pulled me in. He held his shotgun at waist level. Above his dark sunglasses I saw the scar across his forehead, a hairline of red skin and wrinkles.

"I'm walking out of here," Sam yelled as he side-stepped closer to the exit opposite John and me.

John kept the pistol on him. I held mine but kept it pointed to the ground.

"Where you going to go, Sam?" I asked. "They'll find you. And if you shoot someone it will be murder."

"Tracks all over the place. I can go anywhere," Sam said.

"This is no way to settle things," John said. "A good lawyer and you might not even got to jail."

"If I get charged, I'm off the tracks. They won't let me near the dogs. It has to be this way. The dogs. You can't run a farm another way," Sam pleaded.

I didn't know what to say. All Sam had were greyhounds. I knew what it meant to him to be a dog man.

"Put the gun down," Sam said and moved closer.

"Stop," John yelled.

"Put the gun down," Sam said real slow. "I will shoot someone!"

John lowered the pistol some, but it wasn't enough. I could see it as well as Sam.

Then Sam turned. It was a second of movement where the barrel of the shotgun raised, then exploded. And Cathy was left standing there with the leash in her hand. He'd blown Torpedo Joe to the ground, a gaping hole in his side. Cathy started screaming. John let the pistol down all the way, and Sam was already running toward the trees.

Cathy fell to her knees and put her hands on the wound in the dog and kept saying, "No." I tried to put my hand on her shoulder and stop it, but it was useless. Sam was a killer. The dogs meant nothing to him.

"Let him go," John said. "Here comes Block."

I looked toward the trucks and saw Block standing just outside of the trees with a shovel in his hands, and just behind him a cameraman with a big 62 on the side. Cathy stood and wiped her bloody hands on her shirt. She looked at me, then walked toward the rows of cages.

"Cathy," I said, but she kept going.

She reached out and pulled open a cage, and the greyhounds bolted out like they were wild. And in a way they were kept wild so they'd run. The dogs whipped past me and John, and neither one of us made a move to catch them. Pretty soon, she had more cages opened and didn't look like she would stop. John shook his head and chuckled and started toward the field where Block was looking for the hole.

By then, I watched all those greyhounds running through the field in little packs. They headed for the trees, and Don Block looked up, surprised, wondering what to do, and John said something and they went for the hole. I couldn't help but smile. I knew I'd have to go catch those dogs soon, and I promised myself I'd make sure every one was taken care of. I looked back to the cages, and they were all open and she was sitting on the cement with a young hound that wouldn't run. I walked over and stood there and didn't say anything.

"I was wrong, Legget," she said. "I didn't think Sam ..." she tried to say but choked up.

"I know. You had to find out for yourself. It's all right, Cath. It's all going to work out. Where's Fielding?"

"I don't know. Don't try and find him. He'll kill you. I know it."

But I knew where he was. Dexter's Field. And I knew John wouldn't go after Fielding. All he wanted was the farm, and the rest would be handled by the judge. But I felt different. Fielding could get out of it somehow. And I needed to look the man in the eye, to clean him out of my blood.

Chapter 16

Then I saw Scott Road. Fielding's hospital was around the corner. When I pulled into the parking lot, I saw his Honda and another car that must be for the tech and the greyhounds in the cage outside. The hounds went to the edge of the fence and stuck their noses through it as I walked over. I didn't have anything to give them, so I touched their snouts and said something soft which made their tails wag, and the brindle one got excited and started running around his cage. Maybe the ride had cooled me off. These feelings of the old hospital came back.

I looked over at the glass door, covered with plywood, and knew it would be open. It had always been. I slipped inside and just stood in the hallway a second. He could be anywhere, and I didn't want to surprise him. I went down the hall and checked the back areas where the cages were and where the greyhounds lived, and it was empty.

I moved the pistol in my pants again and went back up the hall toward the office. I didn't hear the television and remembered how I'd busted it. Strange thing about it all was how much I loved this animal hospital. Maybe just because I'd spent so much time here. And before I went through the door, I saw him. He was sitting in his usual spot on the couch. I saw his grey hair and the gold of his glasses.

"Legget," he said when I walked in. He put the glass on the floor, and smiled, but it was a dead smile, like it hurt him.

I shut the door behind me, and looked at the broken husk of the television on the conference table, his briefcase and an open bottle. The whiskey smelled strong, and Fielding looked like he'd been up all night. His shirt was wrinkled and his pants were tangled in his boot.

"Took you long enough," he said as I walked past the other couch and stood in front of him, maybe three steps away.

"What the hell does that mean? You're always talking like everything's supposed to happen like it is and you already know it."

He chuckled. "And?"

"And nothing," I said and took the pistol from my pants, held it at my side. "I used to think you were great, someone I looked up to."

That hurt him. I saw it in his eyes.

"Your mistake, I suppose."

"I'm making a lot of mistakes, but that's over now." I raised the pistol.

"Look at this," he said and straightened his pants, pulling the cuffs out of his boot and smoothing it down.

"You burned my trailer. You killed my dog. You used me to get back at your ex-wife," I said more to myself than anyone.

His face turned red. I watched him squeeze the end of the couch and flex his jaw. My fingers started to sweat around the handle of the gun.

"You naïve son of a bitch! Do it!" Fielding was off the couch and in front of my face, spit shooting from his mouth.

And what happened was this: all the anger over my dog's dying and the cruelty and craziness of Fielding seeped away when I saw a man in front of me who was weak and useless and desperate to die. A man too cowardly to end his own miserable ways. I couldn't kill a man like that.

"Take it," I said, my voice calm. I tossed the pistol on the couch next to where he sat. "Kill me, Doctor. Because if you don't ..."

Fielding looked at the pistol. His lips trembled. He looked at me and took it. His eyes pinched up with thought, then he shoved me back. I hit the table, and it skidded, and the bottle crashed against the floor. The reek of whiskey hit me seconds later.

Fielding raised the pistol, pointed it over at me, and I forced myself to breathe slow and long breaths. I thought then, with the pistol bearing down on me, that I was a better man than Fielding and he knew it, maybe he'd known it longer than I ever did.

As I was pulling my hands free of the glass, ready to get up and take it, the explosion of the pistol pushed me back down. My head went black, but I was still thinking, as if one second I was moving and the next I'd fallen into darkness, not knowing how. I tried to stand again, but there was a pain in my side that held me down. I moved my hand there gently, pulled it back sopped in blood. Bastard finally did it, I thought and let myself fall back to the floor. I was in a dream. Moving through scrub oak, my rabies pole catching on branches and fronds, and so much noise like bees or running water in my head. I was thinking, it's all different now. If I lived I'd have a chance to make up for Cal. All the animals that passed through my hands. I was just thinking of all the animals and what I could do.

Somewhere far away, another shot, the clatter of things around me, movement, voices. I was too far away to know what. I couldn't put the sequence together. Then I felt hands, the wincing pain in my side. Someone's fingers there and pressure. I opened my eyes, cloudy with liquid and waves of dark. It was John. I saw him above me, teeth clenched, sweaty face, heaving chest.

"Fielding," I said.

"Son of a bitch shot himself, Legget. Take it easy. You're gonna be fine, just a .22 in the side."

That song of a voice and my dream of catching animals. It would never be the same if I lived. It would be better. I would be a new man, I promised maybe myself, maybe John, who put me down on the floor and left my vision. And maybe it was finally over. Maybe I could go back to the streets.

I closed my eyes and saw a road at dusk broken with pools of yellow sand and a ditch behind it, the grass long-waving and green from rain and sewage and then a hobbled line of pine trees with sparse, dry branches. The road was silent and empty except for me leaning against my truck with muddy boots and sweating. Below the trees I saw eyes lit up like colored jewels, green orbs and red slants and the cautious movement of dogs, hundreds of them, hiding in the trees, looking out at the world. An army of animal souls waiting in the trees for me to breathe.